Murder on Tour

A Lacey James Mystery

PATRICIA DICKISON ELLIOTT

Copyright © 2014 Patricia Elliott
All rights reserved.

No part of this book may be reproduced or transmitted or transferred in any form or by any means, graphic, electronic, mechanical, including photocopying, recording, taping or by any information storage retrieval system or device, without the permission in writing by the author

Any resemblance to actual people and events is purely coincidental.

This is a work of fiction. Names, characters, places and incidents are the products of the author's imagination and are used fictitiously. Any resemblance to actual events or locale, are products of the author's imagination and are used fictitiously.

Paperback-Press
an imprint of A & S Publishing
A & S Holmes, Inc.

ISBN: 1505904951
ISBN-13: 978-1505904956

DEDICATION

Dedicated to Clif who always supported my desire to write.

TABLE OF CONTENTS

Dedication iv
Acknowledgments..i
Chapter 1 1
Chapter 2 11
Chapter 3 25
Chapter 4 37
Chapter 5 46
Chapter 6 54
Chapter 7 65
Chapter 8 70
Chapter 9 74
Chapter 10 82
Chapter 11 90
Chapter 12 100
Chapter 13 114
Chapter 14 119
Chapter 15 124
Chapter 16 128
Chapter 17 136
Chapter 18 145
Epilogue 150
About the Author..152

Acknowledgments

Thanks to my family for their love and for gently laughing at Mom when she obsessed about Ireland, clues, cemeteries and castles.

Thanks also to Sleuths' Ink Mystery Writer group for inspiration, encouragement and friendship.

Aleta Harris, my daughter, thank you for the perfect cover design for Murder on Tour. I love it.

CHAPTER 1

Speakers blared announcements of incoming flights from exotic places, people ran to catch planes, cell phones pressed to their ears, pulling luggage or children behind. The airport tram beeped as it sped down the concourse. Excitement was contagious and Stella and I were excited. Chicago was the first leg of our grand tour of Ireland. Here we will board American Airlines flight 235 non-stop to Dublin.

I looked like I hadn't stopped running since my alarm went off at 5 a.m. Stella was her cool, confident self. A.P., Ardith Percell that is, didn't give us much time to prepare when she called and coerced me into taking this trip to Ireland. Oh, don't get me wrong. I was happy to take the trip. I just wasn't sure I trusted that A.P. was telling me the truth. She could be cagey when she wanted things to go her way.

A.P. is my agent. She is the reason Stella and I

are on this trip. I am Lacey James, writer extraordinaire. Well, not extraordinaire. I'm just an ordinary writer enjoying my work.

Forty-eight hours ago I was on my second cup of coffee, editing and holding my head, trying to understand some of A.P.'s suggestions for the manuscript I had sent last week. When the phone rang, the ID showed it was A.P. calling. When I answered I knew she wanted something because she called me 'Honey.'

"Honey, how is the manuscript coming?"

"I'm working on it now."

"Great. I know you'll have it in on time, you always do. Honey, I need a huge favor."

"Sure A.P. What can I do for you?"

That is when she began to talk fast and wheedle. "Honey, my mother had a heart attack. She is in the hospital and I can't leave her. She and I had tickets to visit Ireland with her sister, AnnaLise. Aunt Anna just got married and the lovebirds decided to honeymoon in Ireland. They planned on tracking down some old family records and maybe even meet some of our Irish connections. Of course, Momma can't go and I can't leave her."

"I'm sorry A.P. …"

She didn't even let me finish before continuing.

"Honey, I want you to go to Ireland for me and look out for Aunt Anna. We haven't met her new husband and we are afraid he means to do her harm. She has a little bit of money and she is susceptible to his suggestions. You get the picture. I just want someone nearby while she is in Ireland."

"A.P. I don't even know your aunt."

"Please, Lacey. You are the only one I can depend on at this point. The trip is all expenses paid. It wouldn't cost you a cent and you might find some ideas for a new book."

"No A.P. I've got galleys to edit and I need to start the second in the series."

"You can edit while on this trip. This is Auntie's honeymoon and for her the trip of a lifetime. There is no way I can talk her out of it. I just want the old dears to have a responsible person they can turn to if they need help. This is very important to me Lacey. Don't let me down."

She was down to begging and what could I say?

"A.P. will you include your other ticket so I can take a friend with me? Two chaperones are better than one."

"I'll do anything you want, Honey. Thank you. Thank you. Hey, take Stella with you. Tell her I will take another look at her proposal for a photography book . I'll send two tickets by overnight mail. Pack your bags; you'll be leaving in two days. I will forever be in your debt."

"Two days? A.P. ...?" But she had already hung up.

I immediately called Stella and did a little wheedling myself. Stella and I have traveled before and we get along great. After a little coaxing, Stella agreed to become a chaperone and accompany me on the trip. She was happy to visit the Emerald Isle on A.P.'s dime.

Our flight from Springfield was late. As soon

as we landed, Stella took off like Moody's Goose with me a couple of strides behind her. She walks fast and I have short legs. The distance between us lengthened, so I secured my carry-on bag on my shoulder, held on to my purse and ran to catch up.

Sorry about the Moody's Goose thing. That is one of my failings as a writer. My country lingo follows me into the mystery and historical books I write. I sometimes get away with it in the historicals, but the younger set doesn't understand my outdated clichés in the mysteries. A.P. keeps me on the straight and narrow in that department but, forgive me, they sometimes pop out of my mouth.

"Are we going to a fire?" My breath came in short gasps.

"Hmm?"

"Are we going to a fire? You're walking so fast I can't keep up."

"Sorry. I just naturally walk fast. I'll try to slow down."

"Well, if you lose me, stop somewhere and wait for me to catch up. OK?"

She smiled in an amused way and kept right on racing down the concourse. I've known Stella for over twenty years in the business world. That was before her husband died and I moved to Oklahoma. Now that we're both retired and widowed, we have become good friends. Good enough to travel together anyway and that is saying a lot about friendship.

"Are we there yet?" I huffed and puffed and moved my little feet as fast as they would go.

"I think it's around this corner," she said, never

slowing down.

"One of those rolling carry-on bags would be nice. My bag is getting heavier by the minute."

"Do you want to stop for a while?"

"No, I'll…" the words were not out of my mouth when a body hit me from behind and sent me sprawling. The purse went one way, the bag another and the oaf that hit me kept on running.

I don't mind telling you I lay there in shock for a long minute before I even tried to move. Spread-eagle on a dirty airport floor is not my idea of a vacation. My possessions were scattered. I was humiliated beyond belief. Stella ran back to help me up. A couple of other people began to gather my things. Stella and a teen with a staple in his lip got me to my feet and helped me totter over to a chair. People picked up my scattered bits and pieces and stuffed them back in my bags. At least, I trusted they were putting them all away.

Stella grabbed my wallet and airline ticket and thrust them into my hands. She continued to gather other things and to thank those helping. I could hear a baby crying somewhere. That's what I felt like doing.

A man hurried up looking worried. "Are you O.K.? Can you walk? Did you hit your head?"

"Yes, yes, and no."

"I'm with airport security. We need to be sure you aren't injured."

"He only hurt my pride." I think I managed a feeble smile. Even in my weakened condition, I noticed this man was very good looking. His gray shirt and tie matched the touch of gray in his dark hair. He didn't look like my idea of airport security, but what do I know?

A scuffle further down the hall caught our attention. The man reacted and walked away even as he said, "I think they have apprehended the man who hit you. I must go. I'll check with you later." And he was off to check out the commotion. Stella was sitting beside me, brushing the dust off my shirt when two couples approached.

"Better check for your passport," one of the men said. "These jerks sometimes use a distraction like that to steal passports."

I scrambled through my purse, bringing up tissues, a comb, my journal, a map of Ireland and a jumble of writing pens, safety pins, paper clips, and more tissues. A compact and lipstick was at the very bottom. I finally remembered that my passport was safely tucked in a pouch around my neck under my blouse.

"We noticed your carry-on bag is an Experience Europe Tour bag," one of the ladies said. She was a large boned woman with short red hair. She was a natural redhead but time had faded the red. Her beautician had helped a bit but faded red showed at the roots. She had an amiable air about her but her speech was short and brusque.

"Are you scheduled on the Ireland Tour?"

"Yes," I acknowledged, bringing my Experience Europe carry-on bag closer to my body.

"We are too," four voices echoed at once.

"We're catching American Airlines flight 235."

Two men and two women, friends no doubt, began to talk about seeing my humiliating fall and what they thought of the man who ran into me.

My head was spinning. I pleaded the need to clean up, and escaped to the bathroom with my purse and carry-on.

My hands shook as I made my way to the sink. The mirror reflected messy hair, my shirt showed a dirty streak down the front and across the shoulder. My face and hands had not escaped the dirt from the floor of the airport either.

I took a paper towel and wiped my burning face and dirty hands. The same paper towel took off a little bit of the dirt on my shirt but I still looked like I'd spent the night in a homeless shelter. A quick comb through my hair, use of the compact and lipstick helped a little bit. I repacked my purse and tackled the carry-on bag. I was embarrassed to know that strangers had handled my unmentionables now stuffed into the bag. The tour booklet advised bringing a change of underwear, deodorant, etc. in case your checked luggage was lost.

I packed everything back in, putting my camera on top and my Tootsie Rolls next to it. Speaking of chocolate, I needed a few in my pocket for the immediate future. In fact, I wished I had a huge chocolate bar to eat right then. That would calm the shakes.

I joined Stella and our new friends looking a bit more tidy but still shaky.

Lacey, this is Andy and Jo Fletcher and their friends, Vernon and Maureen Hancock. They are from Georgia."

"Lacey James," I said as I shook hands all

around.

Maureen was the redhead that had spoken earlier. Her husband Vernon was much older than she. A July-December marriage I thought. The size of the ring on her finger told me he had money.

The Fletchers looked a lot alike. They both carried a few extra pounds; both were dressed in denims and tee shirts. Hers had some kind of cute picture on it.

We gathered our belongings and drifted toward the correct gate for outgoing flight 235. I was glad to sit down and calm myself.

We arranged ourselves in the uncomfortable seats. A mother with three children sat opposite us, sharing a sandwich and soda. The children alternately stared and whined. I sympathized with the woman herding three children to wherever. I wanted to whine a little bit myself.

The airport's loud speaker interrupted my musings. "All outgoing flights are being delayed. The airport is on 'shut-down' until further notice."

A collective groan went up from the group around us and speculation was rampant. Fear in the eyes of a few was catching and several people ran to the ticket counter to find out what was wrong.

Andy Fletcher came back to our group to report, "They're not saying what the problem is; only they assured us it is not a bomb threat."

"As if they would tell us there was a bomb," Maureen's loud voice carried even in the noisy airport. The children reacted by crowding around their mother, spilling the soda.

"It doesn't matter," I muttered to Stella, "we're

not going anywhere bomb or no bomb."

After several minutes, that chocolate craving became stronger. "I'm going to find a candy bar somewhere," I said to Stella. "Do you want something?"

"Maybe a bottle of water." She always makes me feel guilty about eating chocolate and drinking sodas, and my guilt was right there in plain sight around my waist.

I ventured out to find a concession stand while Stella guarded our bags. I felt better after consuming the chocolate and an icy Sprite. That taken care of, we waited some more.

"That guy from airport security never returned, did he?" I put the candy wrapper in the trash can.

"I'm sure you are not as important as what is going on elsewhere in the airport," Stella said with a smile and I knew that was about as close to a joke as she ever got. However, I didn't think it was all that funny.

About an hour later, they began calling flights and ours was one of the first. Gratefully we gathered up our bags and boarded. The plane was full and excitement was high as passengers bustled to find seats, stow luggage and get comfortable. It would be a long overnight to Dublin.

I settled back in my seat as excited as a child before Christmas, but it wasn't sugarplums dancing in my head. I dreamed of thatched cottages, rock fences and Irish dancers.

As usual, I said an unspoken prayer asking God to bless our flight. My mind went to my late husband, Ben. We had talked often of traveling to

Ireland. His death cut our plans short.

One thing he said to me before he died was, "I hope you dance."

A smile lifted my lips at the memory. That was one of our favorite songs, but it is hard to dance without your lifelong partner. Slowly, I was learning to get out of the rut of widowhood and experience new things without Ben. It took determination. Traveling overseas without Ben was one of those learning experiences. He had always taken care of things like lifting luggage, tickets and tipping porters. Now I was on my own.

Squaring my shoulders, I silently promised Ben and myself, I was ready to dance.

Chapter 2

Ireland greeted us with weeping skies. We craned our necks to see mist-shrouded buildings, trees and airplanes before we glided into Dublin Airport. Stella and I did our usual follow-the-leader race to baggage claim with me quick-stepping and gawking at the signs and people around me. I noticed a few aching muscles, no doubt from the fall the day before, but I tried not to show it. At the first water fountain, I downed a couple of ibuprofen.

The luggage carousel yielded one bag each and we rolled on out of the airport to a covered area where we saw a small sign "Experience Europe Tours." The man behind the sign could have been a grumpy leprechaun if he had been shorter. He had a round face and a belly that rested over his belt. His smile was not welcoming. In fact, he did not smile at all. We stood looking at him waiting for directions and he never moved a muscle.

Our friends from Georgia joined us along with a few others with identifying "Experience Europe" carry-on bags. A man claiming to be the tour guide rescued us. He was bigger than the leprechaun, dressed in a suit and tie. He greeted us with what passed for a smile. That should have been our first clue that something was wrong. We didn't spend money to come to Ireland to be greeted with a pasted on smile. He herded us into a group with instructions to wait for other members of the tour.

We waited and we waited, growing more restive and chilly in the damp air. A television in the nether regions kept repeating Heathrow Airport, Americans and High Terrorism Alert. But we couldn't see the television or understand all the words. Tension began to grow. Someone came by and instructed us not to acknowledge we were Americans. Wouldn't you know one of our group had a red, white and blue jacket that looked like the American Flag. I must admit Stella and I sort of edged away from her.

When the tour guide joined us again, we rushed to find out what was happening. He pushed us toward the tour bus, and once we were inside, he explained. "Heathrow Airport in London is closed due to bomb threats aboard American. Dublin airport is open but until this is settled, security is tight especially for Americans."

I glanced at my friend. "Stella, is the world going crazy?" Her only answer was a shrug, then the guide continued.

Some of our tour group is stranded in Heathrow and I'm trying to get in touch with them now.

Please be patient. We will have you to your hotel as soon as possible. In the meantime, I must ask you to stay on the bus."

Mumbles made their way through the bus and I swallowed the lump in my throat. A woman spoke up, her voice was stressed.

"What's going on?"

"We don't know what is happening at this moment and it may not be safe for you to be wandering around. By-the-way," he added with a smile, "Welcome to Ireland. I'm Danny McKinnon, your tour guide."

Stella and I looked at each other. Neither of us voiced our fears. "AnnaLise and Hadley were coming through Heathrow," I said to Stella. "I hope they are alright." AnnaLise King is A.P.'s aunt. Hadley is her new husband.

A few more people trickled into the bus and the grumpy leprechaun loaded their bags into the underneath storage bins. Rain lashed against the windows and we grew colder as we sat wishing we were back in the good old U.S. of A.

Our friend, Maureen from Georgia was especially vocal, first telling everyone how cold she was, then demanding in a raucous voice that husband Vernon find out why we weren't being taken to the hotel.

McKinnon hustled into the bus, apologizing and giving us a little more information than before. "It seems that threats have been made to bomb all U.S. planes leaving Heathrow Airport. That airport is under lock-down. No one is entering or leaving. We have four tour members there and I can't reach them by cell phone. We are not usually so tense. I promise this will not mar your trip."

The tour guide continued his spiel, "Our hotel is the Grand Canal Hotel located, where else but, on Grand Canal Street. I recommend you take time to rest and sleep if you can after your long overnight flight. Our driver is Rory O'Neil. Rory and I have worked together for many years and I guarantee he is the best driver in Ireland.

"At 6 p.m. we invite you to join us for a welcome reception in the hotel bar."

Again, Stella and I rubber necked to see as much as possible as we drove through the narrow streets of Dublin. The rain hindered our view but the excitement returned. We were in Ireland, at last.

The Grand Canal was a modern edifice set among equally modern office buildings and apartments. The lobby consisted of the requisite high desk on one side and chairs for lounging placed at intervals nearby.

A phone message was waiting for me from A.P. The American media would have picked up the story of Heathrow. No doubt it was all over the news. A.P. must be out of her mind with worry. I returned her call even though I knew nothing to ease her mind. She screamed into the phone. "What is going on there? I can't get any answers. Is Aunt Anna with you?"

"Calm down A.P. I don't know anything. I'll phone you the minute I find out where they are. As far as we know, they are still at Heathrow. I can't do anything here. The tour company is making inquiries."

"What is the situation there? No one will tell me anything."

"We aren't getting any information either. Have you called the tour company?"

"Of course, I've called the tour company." She was being sarcastic, but who could blame her? "The tour company, my congress woman and my next call may be to the president."

I knew there was no use trying to reason with her. So I merely said, "We are fine here. Thanks for asking. I'll call you when I know anything." And hung up the phone.

I was relieved to find our room was spacious and clean. Two double beds with snow-white bedding against red and beige walls brightened the dreary day. A spotless bathroom with heated towels reminded me it was more than 24 hours since I'd had a shower.

"Was your phone call from Aunt Anna?" Stella asked.

I slipped off my shoes and collapsed full length on the bed. "No. It was A.P. in a dither calling about Anna and Hadley. I didn't know anything to tell her. Turn on the TV. See if we can find out more about what is happening in London."

She fiddled with the controls and found a news station. They did not give any more information than we already knew.

"I think it is time you told me the whole story about Aunt Anna and Hadley."

"Well, our tickets came with strings attached," I ventured. A.P. is my agent, you know." At her nod I continued. "AnnaLise is A.P.'s aunt. She recently married Hadley King and the family isn't too sure of Hadley's intentions. Anna has quite a lot of money tied up in oil, compliments of her first husband. A.P. and her mother, Anna's sister, planned to come on the tour with the two lovebirds to keep an eye on Hadley and be sure Anna didn't come to harm. Both AnnaLise and Hadley are nearing 80.

"A.P.'s mother had a heart attack and is in the hospital. A.P. didn't feel she could leave her and they had these tickets and . . ."

"And you were chosen to come along and keep an eye on Aunt Anna?"

"You got it. She will not be happy if something happens to Anna on my watch."

"The two of us can keep up with two old people on their last legs. I'll help you. After all, I got a trip to Ireland too."

I appreciated Stella's common sense but in the back of my mind I worried about the two, hoping they got out of Heathrow before the airport closed.

I opted for a quick shower before a nap. Stella continued to try to find news on the television. After my shower, I succumbed to the mind-numbing tiredness of jet lag. When I opened my eyes the bedside clock read 5 p.m.

"I feel better after the nap., I wasn't sure I could sleep after so much excitement."

"I slept a bit but I'm worried about what our children are hearing in the states. They may be worried."

"We need to find a computer and get a message to them via email. Maybe the hotel has a computer in the lobby we can use. I should email A.P. too."

"Look," Stella said gazing out the window. "The sun is shining." Sure enough, the view from our third floor window revealed the sun's rays lighting tiny patio apartments with "Mary Poppins" chimneys in the distance. Pots of flowers bloomed on each patio. It was a storybook scene. We both snapped photos of our first sunlit view of Dublin.

"Can you believe we are in Ireland?"

"We finally made it," she said, with a satisfied smile. "I wish we had time for a walk, but it's nearly time for the welcome party."

"Maybe we should go on down and get acquainted," I agreed. "Although, I'm not looking forward to it. I guess I'll have to act like I'm interested in everyone's small talk."

Stella just grinned at me. She knows me too well. I shook out a pair of beige slacks and a gauze top and stepped into gold colored loafers. My hair is short so a quick brush took care of that. A swish of lipstick, small gold hoop earrings, and I was ready to meet the traveling adventurers downstairs.

The welcome party was in the pub attached to the hotel. Although it was called a pub, it was as modern as any restaurant you would see in a busy American city. Several families were already seated, which you probably would not see in a bar in America.

The Fletchers and Hancocks were already there working on their first cocktail. They, too, had changed in honor of the occasional. It was evident they were seasoned travelers.

"I'll have a soft drink," I said to the waiter who

had beautiful dark eyes and hair. He was young enough to be my grandson, but I could still admire his youth.

"What?" He asked with an accent that was certainly not Irish.

"A soft drink," I repeated.

"Soft drink – I do not know –"

"A Sprite," Danny McKinnon rescued me.

"Oh, Sprite, yes."

"Many of the working young people come from other countries. They are just learning English. Several come from Poland, some from other countries," McKinnon explained. "They come to work and to learn English and also to get an education. The economy is very good here in Ireland and we need the workers."

Two couples came in looking stressed and worried. They were the four who were stranded in London. Hadley and AnnaLise King appeared every bit their age that I knew to be near eighty. She looked frail and ready to collapse. I wondered if they should be traveling at all. Her long curly hair had once been red but now was almost completely gray. I thought it strange that she wore it in the style of a young girl, caught at the crown with a barrette.

Hadley held the floor with his story of being stranded and how a nurse got them out because he became ill. AnnaLise looked like she needed a nurse more than Hadley. He loudly begged our forgiveness for their disheveled appearance as their luggage had not arrived.

The other couple, Matt and Monica Page, was definitely younger than the rest of us. They had arrived from London after hiring a boat to bring them north. They, too, had left without their luggage.

McKinnon hurried to order drinks and snacks for the latecomers. Members of the tour crowded around them to learn of the situation in London. They couldn't add much more than we already knew. It was not the time to introduce myself so Stella and I returned to our table.

Two couples, who said they were teachers, joined us. Their names were Tom and Carolyn Vaughn and Craig and Linda Cranfield from Sioux Falls.

"We're a little green at this," Carolyn confided. "This is our first tour." We exchanged pleasantries including promises to help them with anything they didn't understand. Stella and I are old hands at tours; we travel together every couple of years, though this was our first trip abroad together.

I made my way over to the Kings to get acquainted. Neither of them seemed to recognize my name. Perhaps A.P. hadn't told them of the change of plans. I would take it up with her later.

Happy hour was almost over when the last of our group entered the pub. McKinnon introduced them as Curtis and Rose Edington from Tallahassee, Florida. His hair was snow white but her honey brown hair looked like she had just stepped out of the beauty shop. He carried two glasses of wine while she paused dramatically to survey the room before stepping down the stairs to join us. I got the impression she wanted or expected to be the center of attention. Her black pantsuit cost more than my social security check. She seemed a little feeble or maybe it was tipsy and almost stepped out of her backless heels on the stair. They joined the group with the flair of couples used to relating to strangers. Rose beckoned the waiter and ordered more wine.

Curtis nudged her with one of the glasses he carried. Rose laughed and said, "Oh, Sweetie. I forgot." I don't know if she was talking to her husband or to the attractive young waiter.

After a couple of Sprites and nibbling some chips, Stella and I were anxious to get on with our sightseeing. We decided to walk along Canal Street to find a place for dinner.

The sun was beginning to lower in the sky but we were delighted to find old buildings behind wrought iron fences with bicycles propped on their porches. They were in direct contrast to two-story apartment buildings across the street. Everywhere the flowers were a riot of color in pots and beds.

"Wonderful picture scenes," Stella muttered to herself. Stella's hobby is photography and she has won awards with her unique scenes.

"I want to look at your pictures when we get home. You have such a great eye, while I just point and shoot." I followed my disclaimer by pointing and shooting in every direction.

"I hope the people who live in these apartments know we're just ignorant tourists and do not mean to intrude on their privacy. I think students live in this area, hence the bicycles." I turned to Stella, but I was talking to myself, as she was half-a-block down the street, photographing a weathered iron pot full of petunias.

"You do know we have petunias in Missouri, don't you?" I caught up with her and took a picture of the flowers.

"Shut up and take your pictures. I'll take mine. Okay."

I knew she was joking. At least I think she was joking.

A middle-aged couple strolled along the street meeting us. They seemed mildly amused at the foreigners snapping pictures of everything in sight.

They greeted us with smiles, which gave me the courage to ask, "We're looking for a restaurant for dinner. Is there one this way?"

"No. This is a residential area. There is a hotel on the corner. There is a nice pub there."

The sun was disappearing behind the apartment building when we arrived back at the hotel. The Fletchers and the Hancocks were just leaving along with two ladies who were traveling alone, Billie Owensby from Arizona and Alice Baker from New York State. Billie was middle aged and sturdy. Her no-nonsense jeans and jacket came from the rack at Penny's. Alice looked like she would be comfortable baking cookies for her grandchildren.

"Did you find a place to eat?" Alice asked.

"No, there is nothing this way." .

"Danny told us about a pub around the corner. We are going to try to find it. Want to come along?"

The invitation was welcome and we accepted.

"Let's ask Hadley and AnnaLise to come with us," Billie said. "I'm sure they would welcome a break."

"Sure," said Andy Fletcher. "I'll go get them." He went back inside the hotel and came back walking slowly with Hadley and AnnaLise.

The street followed a tiny stream with humpbacked bridges across it. There were apartment buildings on either side.

"I wonder if it would be safe to be out here after dark," I whispered to Stella.

"Just stay with the group," she whispered back.

At times AnnaLise looked like she couldn't take another step but Hadley pushed her on with a hand in the middle of her back. Billie Owensby walked nearby offering AnnaLise her arm occasionally.

Stella and I trailed along with them several blocks to a picturesque red house set back off the street. A sign proclaimed it "The School House." In its former life, it had been a dwelling now transformed into a restaurant. Painted red with white trim, with a charming walk up to the front door, it sat among carefully landscaped shrubs and flowers.

The restaurant was packed and we quickly found out why it was named, The School House. The crush of young people had to be students. The noise level rivaled the St. Louis Cardinal stadium on game night. Another waiter who didn't speak English escorted us to the balcony where he offered us two couches, two arm chairs and a stool with two coffee tables between them. That was all that was available.

"We're just visiting from America, surely you have something better than this," Maureen protested.

"I am sorry, madam. This is all we have. If madam had reservations. . ."

"We just got here. Oh, all right." Maureen made a moue and chose an armchair.

Everyone ordered salmon except Jo Fletcher and me. I ordered a rib eye. Fish is a staple in Ireland. I don't care for fish and will not eat it unless coerced. Jo ordered a hamburger and fries.

I sat back and let the conversation flow around me. I was soaking in atmosphere. We had to speak loud to be heard above the noise from downstairs. From the bits of sentences, I learned Hadley had been in the military. He was quick to tell us that he and AnnaLise were on their honeymoon. He said they had been high school sweethearts but each had married other people. They had only recently met again and decided to marry.

Alice confided that she often traveled alone. Her latest adventure had been a tour to Alaska and she was planning a trip to Greenland in the near future. The Hancocks and Fletchers conversed about their adjoining apartments, their golf adventures and previous tours. They had a list of places they planned to visit.

Eating was an experience. When I saw Jo Fletcher's hamburger, I regretted ordering the rib eye. A bib would have been handy because bending from a couch to the coffee table to take a bite was an experience in silent prayer. "Please God; don't let me dribble anything on my shirt."

Maureen complained her salmon was overdone but everyone else thought the meal was excellent. While waiting for the ticket we had time to observe the occupants of the pub. The lower floor was full of milling and moving bodies.

I wasn't expecting to see a familiar face but the man eating alone at the corner table looked familiar. Was it the airport security guy who had spoken to us in Chicago? It couldn't be. Could it?

"Stella, that man at the corner table looks like the guy from airport security. Can you see him?"

"Why would he be here?" She searched but the people between kept shifting and moving. "I can't see him. You're imagining things, I'm sure."

"Hey, I wouldn't forget a good-looking guy like that," I joked, but felt a bit uneasy.

Chapter 3

The bed was comfortable and morning came too soon, but Ireland beckoned. We were scheduled for a short talk about the country, then a bus tour of the city. "I want to put my toothbrush in my carry-on when we come back here after breakfast," Stella said, as she hurried into the bathroom.

"Good idea. Need to take pills too," I said, dumping a handful of pill bottles into the attractive Experience Europe carry-on that was part of the tour package. "Camera, notebook, pen," I continued to inventory the carry-on. "What else?

"Oh, Tootsie Rolls," I answered myself, putting a generous handful in my pocket before adding to the stash in the carry-on.

The breakfast room was easy to find. The aroma and the noise of people enjoying themselves reached all the way to the elevator. We chose a table where several of our group were already eating and ordered coffee.

"Better order hot water, too. The coffee is strong enough to turn up your toes," someone advised. Truer words were never spoken. After the first sip, we agreed and beckoned the waiter to ask for a pot of hot water.

"I'm sure the kitchen help are muttering, 'Crazy Americans'", I whispered to Stella.

"Just go to the buffet and help yourself," said Maureen in a loud voice. "The selection is wonderful, but you better hurry, there is another tour group queuing up outside.

Breakfast was indeed luxurious. Stella and I helped ourselves to a mouthwatering array of fruits, pastries, eggs, potatoes, ham, which the Irish call bacon, broiled tomatoes, juice, jellies and scones. We headed back to our table with full trays. The Edingtons were just entering the restaurant. Rose was again perfectly coifed. Her killer pantsuit and high-heeled backless sandals made me feel like I had dressed in the dark. Stella and I had both opted for jeans and walking shoes. A rainproof hoodie over a T-shirt was our idea of dressed for anything.

"Good morning," Stella greeted the old couple. Rose hesitated a minute, smiled myopically and stumbled. Stella quickly shifted her tray to one hand and caught the old woman's arm.

"Just a little off my balance this morning," Rose said. "Thank you, dear," Curtis said as he expertly led Rose to a small table, then ordered tea from the waiter.

After breakfast, we obediently went to the talk about Ireland's economy but Stella and I were restless and resented the long-winded economist. This was Ireland and we wanted to see it not talk about it.

Finally, we escaped. The sun was blinding as it hit the windshield of the bus where it waited in front of the hotel.

"Ah, the breeze feels good after being cooped up in that conference room," Stella commented as Danny McKinnon handed us onto the steps.

Maureen and Vernon were seated in one of the front seats, Andy and Jo Fletcher behind them. "I thought he never was going to shut up so we could leave," Maureen complained to anyone who would listen.

Stella and I worked our way about halfway back. "You take the window seat," I offered, "and we'll switch later."

"Sounds like a plan." Stella settled her carry bag beneath her feet. "I don't know if we'll need this windbreaker or not, but better be safe than sorry, I guess."

"I can put them in the overhead, just hope we don't forget them."

"We won't forget them if it rains."

I looked to see if she was joking. She wasn't. Stella seldom jokes.

McKinnon entered the bus and counted heads. I was surprised to see the tour guide dressed in a suit and tie. Most of the men on the tour wore casual clothes. "The Kings will not be joining us today," he said. They are recuperating from their experience yesterday. They were lucky to get out of Heathrow. We're told planes are still being held at the airport.

No air travel is leaving for America at this point. You should have no trouble leaving Ireland when your tour is finished. Be aware as you shop, stringent rules are being put in effect for carry-on items and your outgoing luggage will be thoroughly searched."

"Well, I'm a fine body guard," I commented to Stella. "Do you think I should stay here with them?"

"I'm sure they need to rest. You can check on them as soon as we return."

"We are two short," McKinnon said. "Who is missing?" he asked of no one in particular. Then answered himself, "The Edingtons."

Just as McKinnon descended the bus steps, the Edingtons appeared at the door of the hotel. She, still teetering on her tiny high heels, carried only a tiny purse. Mr. Edington clutched her arm and balanced a couple of carry bags.

Rose tripped into the bus with a smile and chose a seat across from Stella and me. Her expensive perfume filled the air.

Meanwhile McKinnon brought a stunning redhead aboard. She was tall and slim, a true Irish beauty with fair skin and blue eyes. She wore a green pantsuit that set off the long red hair cascading around her face.

"We have a surprise today." McKinnon's brogue surfaced a bit when he introduced her. Could he be nervous or was he putting on a show? "Sure and this Lassie is Irene Bouchard, joining us as a trainee guide. 'Tis true and anyone will tell you, Rory and I are the best teachers in the business. Ms. Bouchard canna go wrong with us."

The lady dipped her head to us and took the seat McKinnon offered behind the flip down seat provided for the guide.

McKinnon took a stance with a microphone facing us as Rory pulled the bus away from the curb. "We'll be taking a quick tour of Dublin this morning with a stop at St. Patrick's Cathedral, then Trinity College to view the Book of Kells."

Dublin flew by as we tried to see it all from the huge bus windows. We glimpsed elegant Georgian houses built in late 1700 and early 1800's, their graceful arched doorways crowned with leaded windows. McKinnon pointed out the Lord Mayor's home and pubs on Duke Street.

"I'd like to stop and take a few pictures," Stella mourned as we flew by the beautiful buildings surrounding St. Stephen's green, while McKinnon recounted the 1916 Easter Rising.

My interest centered on the bookstores on Dawson St. But tours do not cater to individuals and I hoped I could find a way later to visit at leisure.

I caught my breath in awe as the bus drew up in front of St. Patrick's Cathedral. McKinnon gave a quick rundown of the history of the famous cathedral. It is one of the oldest buildings in Dublin. Thinking of the history those walls have known made me long for my laptop.

"I read the history of St. Patrick last winter," Stella confided.

"You read history?" I pretended to be amazed. "I thought you only read the financial pages."

Her laugh told me I had hit a nerve and she understood my joke and was beginning to enjoy the trip.

"Look, do you want me to tell you about St. Patrick or not?"

"Yes, tell me about St. Patrick." I struggled to get my camera out of my pocket as we exited the bus beside the archaic fence surrounding the cemetery. Then I plastered my nose against the fence to get a picture of the large Celtic cross monuments inside the enclosure.

"St. Patrick is the patron saint of Ireland. He was brought to Ireland as a slave when he was about 16 years old. He escaped and returned later as a missionary."

"You did read that book!"

"I'm not telling you another thing until you quit teasing." The tour group scattered to various parts of the cathedral. I passed by the gift shop with its postcards and Celtic cross jewelry, but grabbed a brochure telling the history of the cathedral and identifying the tombs of those buried within the walls and floor of the structure. Stella was already aiming her camera at the high arched columns. My gaze wondered to the beautiful stained glass windows. As I snapped picture after picture, I wondered if I would remember what each subject was. I decided I should get out my journal and take a note or two about the photo subjects.

I paused reverently at St. Patrick's statue. I stepped back to focus my camera and stepped on Irene Bouchard, the trainee tour guide.

"I'm so sorry," I murmured. She was standing so close behind me I couldn't turn to apologize.

The smile she gave me was cold like I was in a

place I shouldn't be. "Quite alright, Luv." I didn't think Luv was a term of endearment.

"May I take your picture with the great man's statue?"

"How nice of you to offer." I relinquished my camera and we did the usual pose, say cheese and click. She was still standing there when I strolled away.

I wandered around the enormous old church in awe of the furnishings, the tombs the statues and the beautiful floor tiles.

I saw Stella. She had her camera aimed at some tarnished armor on the wall. I beckoned to her. "Look at these floor tiles. Can you believe all the colors? Think of all the feet that had walked over them."

"Did you see the Jonathan Swift's tomb," she asked? His friend Stella is buried near him. He was Dean of St. Patrick's and he also wrote *Gulliver's Travels,"* she gushed.

My excitement matched hers. My words tumbled over each other. "I saw it. Stella's real name was Esther Johnson. Her nickname was Stella. I think I got a good picture. Way back there in the corner are two Celtic stone grave slabs that have Christian symbols."

"And your writer's imagination is in full gear," she said. "You'll be up all night writing."

"No, I promise I won't do any writing on this trip, but I plan to take a lot of notes. Look at that old door. I wonder what it is."

We took pictures of the door, aged and blackened but with a vertical hole cut in the center.

The legend told us it is the Chapter Door commemorating the peaceful end of a feud between the Earl of Ormond and Earl of Kildare in 1492. The Earl of Kildare cut a hole in the door and reached his arm out to grasp the hand of his enemy, Ormond.

"I couldn't help overhearing," Irene Bouchard interrupted. "You're a writer? Have I read anything you've written?"

Was she following me?

"Probably not. I write mysteries and historical novels. I doubt if you would find them here in Ireland."

"How exciting to meet a real author. Always thought I'd like to write a book someday. By the way, do you have a piece of paper and pen I could borrow?"

I laughed and tore out a sheet from my notepad. "Are you going to start writing that book right now?" I dug into my purse. "Everything goes to the bottom of my purse."

Stella fished a pen out of her pocket. "I have an extra."

"Thanks," Bouchard wrote something on the paper and handed the pen back.

"Keep it until you get another one," Stella offered.

"I'll return it when we get back to the bus." As Bouchard turned away, she said, "I can't believe a writer carries only one pen."

I looked at Stella and lifted my eyebrows.

We got back on the bus for a short ride to Trinity College. Funny how people migrate to the same seats all the time. Rose and Curtis settled themselves across from us bearing cards and souvenirs. "I could stay in there all day," Rose chirped.

McKinnon took up the microphone and began to tell us about our next stop. "We will be stopping next at Trinity College, founded in 1592 by Elizabeth I to save the Irish from becoming Catholic. The Book of Kells, located on the campus, is a medieval manuscript that was printed and illustrated by hand by monks on the Isle of Iona in the 6th century.

"Where is the Isle of Iona?" someone asked.

"Iona is a small island off the west coast of Scotland. It is known as the Cradle of Christianity. The Book of Kells was produced there before Vikings raided the island."

You are free to tour the campus, view the Book of Kells and explore Dublin. Meet the bus at 5 p.m. for a ride back to the hotel. Have a nice day and enjoy Dublin."

We joined a long line of tourists outside the library at Trinity College. The line shuffled into a vast room with shelves reaching to the lofty ceiling. We formed two lines on either side of the covered case and looked down to view the ancient manuscript. There was no time to stop and gaze with awe as the person beside you or behind you was pushing to see as much as possible. I took time to gaze into the shelves and wondered what other treasures were housed there.

Back out into the courtyard, we pulled our jackets around us. It was beginning to mist a bit and the wind was more than chilly. We looked around to get our bearings.

"Let's find a pub for lunch and then look for a bank to change some traveler's checks. I don't have many euros left," Stella said.

"Sounds good to me. Any ideas how to get off the campus?"

"No. Let's go through those buildings over there and see if that is a way out."

"Hi, ladies." It was Irene. "If you're looking for a sandwich, the school has a snack area. Danny told me it will be cheaper and quicker than a pub at this time of day."

"Lead on, McDuff." I need to learn to be a friendlier person. She's really just trying to help, I thought. There was something about her that just rubbed me the wrong way.

The snack bar was crowded with students, but service was quick. "Do you see any tables?" I asked.

"They all seem to be full. I guess we'll just have to wait a while."

"We could sit on the stairs, like those kids," I ventured.

"If I get down there, you'll probably have to help me up." Stella grinned.

"Come on, pal. I'll boost you up, if I can get up myself.

We sank down together and Irene perched on a stair above us. We listened to the accents and languages around us and watched the students as we munched the apples we had purchased.

"I think I need a something sweet," Stella said

as she wiped her hands on a napkin.

"I have Tootsie Rolls," I said, reaching beside me for my purse only to find Irene's hand hovering over it. "Oh, sorry," she apologized. "I thought that was mine. I have my eye on one of those chocolate bars." She grabbed her purse and went toward the snack bar.

"If I didn't know better, I'd think she was about to put her hand in my purse." .

"It did look that way, but she said she thought it belonged to her."

We need to find a bank before we plan to do any sightseeing."

"O.K. I'm ready," I said, gathering my bag and putting on my jacket.

We didn't have to go far to find the Bank of Ireland. It was a beautiful building which we learned was formerly the House of Lords.

Stella did her financial magic while I stood by looking like I knew what I was doing. Fortunately, Stella knew about dollars and euros and got us safely though the lines.

Then the Dublin streets did their magic. Again, we were transported into a place we never thought we would see. We sighed, pointed and snapped pictures of buildings, churches and street scenes, always mindful of street names so we could find our way back to Trinity College to catch the bus. Words like awesome and thrilling bubbled up without our being conscious of saying them.

My camera was focused on a church at the end of a narrow street when I felt a tug on my arm. I turned and was pulled along the street before my purse left my arm.

I saw the young ruffian who took it sprinting away. Stunned I couldn't say anything for a minute. Then screamed, "He took my bag. Stop him."

I got some attention but the young man kept on running. I ran after him, yelling, "Stella, he took my purse." But I was no match for the fleet-footed thief.

Then I saw someone take him down with a flying tackle. They wrestled for a while before the young man escaped. Stella and I ran up just as the tackler stood up, my bag in his hand.

"That's my purse," I exclaimed.

"I know, I've been watching him. He targeted the two of you when you came out of the bank." He handed my blue bag back to me intact. "He didn't have time to take anything."

"Thank you so much. If I had lost this... Hey, I know you. You are on our tour."

"Yes, Matt Page. This is my wife Monica." He indicated a woman standing nearby.

"Are you alright?" Monica inquired. "He didn't hit you did he?"

"I'm Lacey James and this is my friend, Stella Gerritson. He didn't hit me, just grabbed the bag. My arm may be sore, he jerked pretty hard. Thank you so much. How can I repay you? Could I buy you and your wife a soda or something?"

"No need. I'm glad to be able to help. We're on our way back to Trinity College to catch the bus back to the hotel. Why don't you come with us? I don't think that guy will try anything.

Chapter 4

AnnaLise and Hadley were sitting at a small table in the courtyard when the bus arrived at the hotel. The mist had cleared and the late evening sun touched the couple as they sat holding hands. Stella and I rushed over to speak with them "How are you feeling?" I asked. "I hope you were able to rest?"

"Sister, believe me. It was a horrendous experience. We were trapped in that airport and didn't know what was happening. They wouldn't tell us anything." Hadley was off again telling the same story he had told several times last evening.

"But how are you feeling now?"

"I would feel better if we had our luggage," Anna replied.

"Now, now, sweetheart," Hadley patted her arm. "They said the luggage would be here this evening, just in time for you to get all dressed up for dinner. You'll be the prettiest girl there."

"A.P. called last night. She was worried about you." I said.

"A.P.? A.P.? Who did you say?" Anna asked a puzzled look on her face.

"Your niece. A.P."

"She hasn't got a niece named A.P.," Hadley said. "Come on AnnaLise. Let's go lie down awhile before dinner. Maybe our luggage has arrived." He urged her from the table and into the hotel.

"What do you make of that?" I asked Stella.

"It is strange that she doesn't acknowledge A.P. or even seem to recognize the name."

"I think I need to call A.P."

"Email would be cheaper," Stella advised.

"You're right. But I think I need to talk to her."

I went to the desk to put through a call to A.P. while Stella went on up to the room. After a long wait to get through, I had a short discussion with A.P. After that, I was more than happy to retreat to my room and solitude.

But solitude was evasive. "What did A.P. say?" Stella wanted to know.

"She wasn't happy. I woke her from a sound sleep. She said Anna doesn't know her as A.P. Anna knows her niece as Ardeth Anne. She is named after Anna, by-the-way. We decided it best not to explain to Anna, but that I will continue watching out for her."

"That is a great title for a book, *The Anonymous Bodyguard,*" Stella snickered.

"That is just the way I would write it too, anonymously."

Our room was made up and it was inviting to flop

down and put my feet up. All too soon, it was time to prepare for dinner.

McKinnon had explained to us that dinner was at the Jurys Doyle Hotel featuring The Burlington Cabaret. Stella and I decided that meant dressing up so we each pulled out the one dress the tour company advised us we would need. Stella's tall figure was elegant in a broomstick skirt of many colors. Her blouse complimented the skirt. She added an American Indian designed squash blossom necklace over her head.

"I love your necklace," I said. "Did you buy it in Arizona when you visited your daughter?"

"Yes, it was too expensive but it goes so well with this skirt, I just had to have it."

"Well, you don't have any other vices so you deserve an expensive piece of jewelry if you want it."

I opted for a basic black with a sassy red silk tee and a dressy jacket. Some modest bling from Wal Mart was all I had to dress it up. "I'm sure my outfit won't come close to Rose Edingtons tonight."

I felt confident as we joined the tour in the lobby, waiting to board the bus. We didn't have to be ashamed of our shopping mall buys. Rose Edington was the only tour member to shine in a gauzy ensemble of teal blue with heels to match. Although Maureen ran her a close second, the woman had rings on every finger and a huge stone of some kind looped around her neck. The ears had not escaped. They sported dangling diamonds.

"She must have brought a shoe store," I commented to Stella, nodding toward Rose. "She has on a different pair of shoes every time I see her."

Stella was making her way toward Hadley and AnnaLise and I followed. When Maureen Hancock stepped in front of me, I had to step behind a mirrored column. That was when I came face to face with the man from the airport. Well, not face to face. More like mirror to mirror. I could see his reflection standing behind a fake tree about 3 yards behind me. He knew I saw him and he scooted into the waiting elevator.

I stared into the mirror, not believing my eyes. Stella discovered I wasn't behind her and came back for me.

"What is wrong with you? You look a little shaky."

"It was him, the man from the airport. I saw him in the mirror. He was standing right over there." I turned and pointed.

"Which man? There's no one there."

"It was the man from airport security. I saw him there behind that fake tree."

"Lacey, you couldn't have seen a man from Chicago O'Hare. You saw someone who looked like him."

"But I thought I saw him at the School House Restaurant last night, remember?"

"You're tired. Clean your glasses and come on. McKinnon is loading the bus."

I followed her reluctantly, still looking behind me.

Both Danny McKinnon and Rory O'Neal had spruced up to attend our dinner. McKinnon was quick with compliments as he handed each lady into the bus. Stella and I spoke to the driver, Rory, as we waited to board the bus. He smiled a small grin and dropped his head.

"I think Rory is a bit shy," I commented to Stella after we found a seat on the bus.

"Yeah, but he's kind of cute."

I looked at her in astonishment. I had never heard her comment on a man's looks in all our years of acquaintance. True she was widowed several years ago but as far as I knew, she never dated.

Our bus pulled into a parking spot in front of the Jurys Doyle Hotel. To our dismay, there were several other buses there also. "This is a popular spot," I murmured to Stella.

McKinnon must have heard me for he said, "You will enjoy the dinner and the entertainment."

He was right. We were not disappointed in either. The only drawback was the crowd. The place was packed. Our chairs were so close together, we could hardly move. Billiee Owensby nearly ran over me to get to a chair next to AnnaLise. The Edingtons sat across from the Kings. A good match, I thought. Curtis is too tired to talk but Hadley won't even notice.

Waiters bustled around filling water glasses and taking drink orders. An engraved menu placed at each setting gave us our choices for dinner. The noise level was deafening as we discussed the several selections. I chose Cream of Fresh Vegetable Soup as my appetizer. It was unlike any I had tasted before but I was not disappointed in my choice. We had a choice of four entrees from the elegant printed menu. The description of Herb Crusted Prime Roast Irish Beef sounded exotic, served with pearl onions, wild mushrooms and green peppercorns. "I'll have the beef," I told the waiter.

Stella had the Grilled Darne of Shannon Salmon, draped (their word not mine) in a rich Celtic Sauce with chopped dill. Believe me we didn't eat like that where we came from. In our hometown, those dishes would more likely to be plain old pot roast and catfish.

We became better acquainted with the schoolteachers from South Dakota as they sat across from us. We learned that Tom Vaughn was a fourth grade teacher and his wife Carolyn taught speech at their local high school. Craig and Linda Cranfield also taught high school subjects. Craig was the basketball coach and Linda taught English.

Craig and Carolyn seemed to sparkle when they smiled at each other. I wondered if anyone else noticed. Stop it, Lacey, I told myself. It's none of your business.

"So how do you like the tour so far?" Stella asked.

"It is wonderful. I loved seeing the Book of Kells," Linda smiled. "I will do a bit of research when I get home and have an interesting lesson for my students."

"I wanted a chance to look at some of the other books in the library," I volunteered. "What did you find interesting today, Tom?"

"St. Patrick's Cathedral was awesome," he replied.

Maureen's, "This wine is cheap and tasteless," interrupted our conversation. "You would think for what we paid for this tour, we could get a decent wine."

McKinnon, ever the genial host, slipped behind our chairs with difficulty because of the number of people dining and produced a wine more to Maureen's taste.

Conversation buzzed up and down the table, with the teachers making private jokes among themselves, Stella and I turned to our other table companions. Billiee was on Stella's right but Billiee was only interested in AnnaLise. Irene Bouchard was to my left. She seemed interested in my life and where I had traveled, questioning me about my family and my writing.

I'm sorry to say, I was at times a bit short with her. I don't like pushy people.

We exclaimed over the entrees with their accompanying vegetables cooked in almond butter. The traditional colcannon was delicious. In this case, it was creamed potatoes with shredded spinach and broccoli. By this time, I'd had enough water to make a trip to the bathroom necessary. I excused myself and walked around the edges of the dining room to the back where the restrooms were located. Several others had the same idea and the line was long. It was hot in the dining room so while I waited I decided to get a breath of fresh air. I slipped out the front door; to find that smokers had so fouled the air that breathing was nearly impossible. Trying to stay away from the smoke, I ventured to the outside of the group.

There was nothing to see as tour buses blocked the view of the city. I turned to go into the dining room, when a rough hand grabbed my arm. Startled, I tried to turn around.

"Don't turn around, missy. I want it now. Give it ter me or ye'll be in big trouble."

Frozen in fear, I said, "I don't know what you're talking about."

He grasped me roughly by both arms and began to shake me. "Oh, ye know what I'm talkin' about. Fer yer own good, give it to me."

I struggled to get away but he only held me tighter. "Please. Let me go. I don't have anything you want."

A man stepped up beside me and put his arm around me. "Are you ready to go back into the dining room, my dear?"

Immediately the hands that held me loosened their grip.

I rubbed my upper arms. I thought I could still feel the ruffian's hands on me. "Thanks," I gasped to my rescuer. Then I looked into his face. It was the man from the airport. I remembered his tall figure, with black hair going to gray. He was impeccably dressed as though he too had been dining in the hotel.

"You! What are you doing here? Are you following me?"

"Yes, ma'am, I am. What did that man say to you?"

"Did you see him?"

"No, it was too dark to see him. I need to know what he said to you."

"And I need to know why you are following me."

"I can explain, but not here. I'll come to your hotel room this evening after dinner. I'll explain everything then. My name is Mitch Logan. Do not go anyplace alone tonight and do not let anyone into your hotel room until I get there. Don't mention this attack to anyone."

He escorted me into the dining room and faded away among the tourists still standing around the door.

Shaken, I went back to my table, all thoughts of a bathroom forgotten.

"You got back just in time for dessert," Stella said. I think the entertainment is about to start. After what I'd just experienced, dessert and entertainment was anticlimactic.

The Fitzwilliam Chantilly looked delicious but I couldn't swallow a bite. When the waiter brought the traditional Irish Coffee of hot coffee, Irish whiskey and double cream, I decided I needed a stiff drink although I'm not a drinker. The drink tasted like they had just waved the whiskey bottle over the coffee and not much dropped in.

Chapter 5

When the show finished, several hundred people surged through the doors leading to the buses. As we pressed together, I felt a bit claustrophobic and a distinct fear of those around me. I clutched Stella's hand like a two-year-old afraid she would lose her mother, all the while glancing around me.

"Are you okay?" Stella asked.

"No, something happened when I went to the bathroom. I can't talk about it now." Around us, people laughed, discussed the show and dinner. All I could think about was the man who threatened me. I was happy to take Rory's hand and scramble into the bus.

"My salmon was cold," Maureen complained. "But we finally got some decent wine."

"Weren't the dancers fantastic?" Carolyn Vaughn gushed. "I've never seen anything like it."

Across from us, Rose leaned against the

window with her eyes closed. Lines of exhaustion creased her face.

Back at the hotel, Stella hurried me to our room. "What in the world happened? You look sick."

"There was a man," I gasped through tears that began to fall. "He threatened me. Stella, I was so scared. Then the man from the airport..."

"Lacey, the man from the airport is in Chicago. He is not in Ireland."

"No, he's here and he is coming to our room tonight." She put her hand on my forehead.

"Do you have a fever? You're hallucinating. Sit down in this chair." I brushed her hand away and mopped tears with my fingers. She rummaged in her suitcase and found tissues. I grabbed several and used one to blow my nose.

"He is here. His name is Logan. The attacker wanted something from me. Look, I have bruises on my arm where he grabbed me."

"This Logan attacked you?"

"No, no. The attacker ran off when Logan acted as if we were together. Then Logan took me inside and said he would come to our room tonight to explain."

"I swear, Lacey. I am never traveling with you again. You attract trouble like a kid attracts dirt."

There was a knock on the door. "There he is. Will you let him in while I wash my face?"

"I will not. I don't know this Logan from Adam. I'm not opening that door."

I scrubbed my face with a tissue, blew my nose again, and wondered if I was doing the right thing. I was shaking when I opened the door.

"Ms. James?" I nodded and stood aside for him to enter. His presence filled the room. He was tall, at least a foot taller than my 5ft. 2, with broad shoulders. He still wore his white shirt from dinner but now unbuttoned at the collar, cuffs rolled up. I noticed his muscular arms before my eyes traveled up to his face. It had a rugged look as if he spent hours in the sun, not handsome but attractive. He had changed into neatly pressed jeans. *How does he keep his jeans so neatly pressed? My jeans look like I got them from the bottom of the hamper.*

"Ms. James, I am Special Agent Mitch Logan with U.S. Homeland Security, formerly with the FBI. I'm sorry to intrude on your vacation but circumstances call for drastic measures. What happened outside the dinner club tonight, Ms. James?"

"Lacey," I said. "My name is Lacey. I don't know what happened. I went out for a breath of air and this man grabbed me from behind. He kept demanding that I give it to him. I don't even know what he meant. If you hadn't intervened, I think he might have dragged me away. Thank you for saving me from serious harm. I'm sorry I know I'm babbling. Still in shock I guess."

Stella put her arm around me. "You are safe now. Forget about it. That man thought you were someone else."

"This is my friend Stella Gerritson."

He shook hands with Stella. Then casually leaned back against the closed door, one hand in the pocket of his jeans.

"I'm afraid we can't forget about it. I followed you here from Chicago. You spotted me a couple of times when I didn't intend for you to see me. I'm glad I was near you tonight."

Stella and I backed up and sat side-by-side on the end of the bed like recalcitrant schoolgirls before the school principal.

"We need to see some identification," Stella demanded.

He produced a leather-covered badge from his pocket. We examined it minutely, although neither of us would know a Homeland Security badge from a kid's toy.

"I don't understand." I ventured. "We're in Ireland; surely you have no jurisdiction here."

"I'm working with the Special Detective Unit of the Irish Garda. We are up against international terrorists. A man named Ben Marshall was murdered in Chicago. Marshall was a double agent. He was carrying a microchip with high security information on it. We're still trying to determine how Marshall got the information out of Quantico. We're not even sure why Marshall carried the microchip to Chicago, but we know his killer took the microchip. The murderer was a small time crook named Clive Gerard. We believe someone hired him to kill Marshall and deliver the microchip to an agent at O'Hare Airport. We followed him to O'Hare, then we lost him. We found him a short time later in a bathroom, bleeding to death from a knife wound. He did not have the microchip on him. Clive Gerard was the man who ran into you as you walked to your concourse to board your plane. We think he may have planted the information on you when he ran into you."

"You don't think I. . ."

"No, we know you aren't part of the extremist cell. They know you aren't either. But they also know you have that bit of information and they want it badly enough to kill for it."

"That is what the man tonight wanted from me? Information?"

"Well, actually, he wanted the microchip his cohort stole from the U.S. government."

"But I don't have anything."

"They think you have it and that makes you a target."

"What is on the microchip?" Stella asked.

"There are thousands of terrorist cells all over the world. We have successfully imbedded agents in some of these cells. We use the information they give us to track activity and possibly stop attacks on U.S. soil and on our allies. The microchip identifies those agents. If our enemies obtain that information, they will murder our agents and we will no longer have the inside information we need to apprehend the criminals before they do great damage."

"How did you pick up our trail so fast?" I wondered aloud.

"When I stopped to help you after you fell, I noticed your Experience Europe Tour bags. It was easy to determine the tour destination was Ireland. I obtained a first class ticket and boarded the plane after you did. I got off the plane before you. I've been following you since you landed."

"And the terrorist, how do they know where we

are?"

"We think they called a cell member here and alerted someone to meet your plane. We know one of the leaders in Ireland is Jimmy O'Shea. He is masterminding the operation to obtain the microchip from you. He is a dangerous man. He should be behind bars but we can't get enough evidence on him for a trial."

"I think we should pack up and go home," Stella said.

"That won't solve the problem. As long as they think you have the microchip they will try to take it from you."

"But I don't have their microchip," I protested.

"Maybe you do and just don't know it. The microchip is small. He could have dropped it in your pocket or in your bag. We're sure Marshall hid the microchip in some kind of container. We just don't know what kind of container. Could we look through your purse and your carry-on bag to see if there is something there that doesn't belong to you?"

"I guess so." To say the least, this strange man wanting to go through my bags was disconcerting, but to think that someone out there would kill me for something I didn't even know I had, scared me to death.

I dumped my purse out on the bed. Out came the usual mess. I can't keep my purse tidy. There was my notebook, wallet, compact, lipstick, and tissues, both used and clean, I was embarrassed to note. I sorted out pens, Ibuprofen, a folder with pictures of my grandchildren, my pocket calendar, some keys, two paperclips, several safety pins, hand lotion, chap stick, passport, and a dozen Tootsie Rolls.

"It could be anything small," he said, bending over the items. "Do all these things belong to you? Please look carefully."

He was so close I could smell his aftershave, a pleasant scent of citrus of some kind. I slumped down beside my junk and reported, "It's all mine."

"What about the carry-on bag? Have you looked in it recently?"

"I carry it with me everywhere we go but I sometimes leave it on the bus when we go inside an attraction. They assured us the bus remained locked." I crammed my things back in my purse and reached for the carry-on bag and dumped the contents on the bed.

His long fingers explored through the brochures, schedules, more Tootsie Rolls, a map of Ireland, a scarf, my small flashlight, digital camera, a comb and my windbreaker. "Why didn't you bring the kitchen sink?" he inquired dryly.

"I couldn't get it through customs."

He looked at me in surprise, then we all laughed rather nervously.

He pulled the jacket pockets inside out dumping out Tootsie Rolls and empty wrappers.

"You like Tootsie Rolls?" he asked, and I detected a hint of another smile.

I smiled sheepishly and admitted I was addicted to chocolate and Tootsie Rolls were my favorite.

I don't find anything here but for some reason El Qaeda thinks you have something they want. Be assured Ms. James –"

"Lacey, please."

"Be assured, Lacey, I'm sticking with you until we catch these people. Wherever you are, I'll be close by."

"That kid that stole my bag today in Dublin, was he with El Qaeda?"

"Yes, he was. We caught him but he wouldn't say a word. He's in a Dublin jail. He didn't have time to take anything from your purse or the man tonight would not have accosted you." He strode to the door. "Good night, ladies. Rest well."

Stella hurried to lock the door behind him. I felt like I was frozen in space. "Did he say, rest well?" I asked. "I don't think I'll ever feel safe again."

Chapter 6

I did not sleep well and woke up tired.

"Don't forget we have to have our suitcases out by 7 A.M. for staff to pickup. We're leaving Dublin today." Stella was entirely too cheerful for my disposition this morning. "The bus will leave at eight."

"I'm running late. I'll just have coffee in the room while I pack," I said. "Bring me something for a snack, would you."

"Sure. I'll see you on the bus."

I had trouble concentrating as I packed my carry-on. I dreaded the day. Someone wants to kill me for something I don't have. I didn't want to step foot outside the door. I grabbed my purse and carry-on and took a quick look around to see if we had packed everything. I trudged to the door and cautiously stuck my head out first. No one in the hall. Hurry, hurry, drag out that suitcase. Hurry,

hurry to the elevator. Shoot! Someone could be in the elevator. Maybe I should take the stairs. Someone could be in the stairway. I should have gone down earlier with Stella.

I gripped my purse and carry-on, and hurried to the elevator. As I pushed the down button, the doors opened to reveal Rose and Curtis Edington. I breathed a sigh of relief and entered.

"Good morning. I think we missed breakfast." Rose welcomed me. "I absolutely had to wash my hair this morning."

"Yes, it's nearly time to catch the bus," I said with a smile. "I had coffee in the room."

"So did I and that is plenty for me, but poor Curtis didn't get breakfast either." Poor Curtis was loaded down with two carry-on bags, plus Rose's coat and purse. Rose looked calm as a beauty queen in her elegant warm up suit and designer tennies. I felt scruffy in jeans I wore yesterday.

I brushed my jeans with a wet washcloth, I thought. In addition, I showered this morning so I don't smell.I didn't take time to blow dry my hair. I felt ratty compared to Rose.

"Maybe we can get some fruit from the buffet for later," I said to Curtis. He just nodded as if he was too tired to do anything else.

We exited the elevator to see many of our group buying newspapers and souvenirs at the gift shop. I moseyed on outside looking for Stella. I was surprised to find her, drinking coffee with the grumpy, shy leprechaun bus driver. She was laughing and he was smiling. He was smiling! Really now!

I turned back inside and began talking to Alice Baker.

"Just buying a newspaper and some mints," she said.

"Have you been on many guided tours?"

"Oh, yes. I go quite often. My last tour was to Alaska and before that I went to Italy."

"Do you always go alone?

"Usually. My daughter works and none of my friends are travelers. They think they are too old to travel alone, but I enjoy meeting new people."

We laughed together as we stepped up behind Andy and Jo Fletcher to get on the bus. They slid into the second row of seats behind Vernon and Maureen Hancock.

Stella sat about halfway back. I dropped down beside her. "I thought maybe you would go for the front seat this morning," I teased.

Mitch Logan entered the bus.

"Maybe you would like me to move," she retorted.

We both snickered.

"Actually, he's really nice," she said.

"Which one?"

She elbowed me and looked out the window as Mitch took the seat behind us.

I didn't know whether to acknowledge him or not so I didn't, but I was very aware of his presence behind me.

Rory settled into the driver's seat and started the bus with a quiet roar of the powerful engine. One good thing about traveling on tours: the buses are quiet and luxurious. McKinnon took his place at the front of the bus with a microphone. Irene Bouchard came running to get on the bus before Rory closed the door.

"She has beautiful hair," I commented to Stella.

"A true Irish beauty," she agreed.

"Top a' tha' mornin' to you." McKinnon was back into his Irish brogue. "I hope you rested well last night after our party at the Burlington Irish Cabaret. The entertainment and dinner was suburb. The best I've seen. You saw some traditional Irish dancing and wasn't the food delicious? I hope you enjoyed it and are ready to see the more rural sights in Ireland now. I want to introduce you to a new person with us this morning. Mitch Logan is in Dublin on business. He had a few days free and asked if he could join our tour."

McKinnon smiled at Mitch who threw up his hand and looked around at everyone.

"What is happening at Heathrow?" someone called.

"Ah, I'm glad you asked. Planes are flying again with very tight security. Airlines are not allowing many items in carryon bags. I'll have a complete list for you sometime today. In the meantime, I suggest you send large purchases home by mail rather than try to take them on the airplane. The shops will gladly help you with that.

"We are leaving Dublin now. On your right, you will see the Ha'Penny Bridge, built in 1816 over the river Liffey. It is called Ha'Penny Bridge because the toll to cross was half a penny. Notice the cast iron railings and decorative lamps."

"I wish we could stop and get a picture," Stella

said, trying to focus through the bus window.

"No doubt, we can find a postcard of the bridge," I said.

"We'll be traveling south from Dublin to County Wicklow, known as the 'Garden of Ireland'."

My mind wandered as McKinnon continued his spiel. I noticed that April Batson had managed to come to sit beside Logan. April is a single woman hailing from Minnesota, traveling alone. What can I say; April is April, a bit ditzy but friendly and fun to be around.

"The countryside is beautiful," I remarked to Stella as we rubbernecked to see cows and sheep grazing in green fields on both sides of the road.

"I see every shade of green in the fields," she said. "I guess that is why they call Ireland 'The Emerald Isle.'"

"The stone fences are just like I've seen in pictures. It all looks so peaceful."

Hadley noticed my word peaceful and commented, "It wasn't peaceful a few years ago. The war between the Catholics and Protestants was not so long ago."

Stella and I ignored him, but Billiee Owensby engaged him in conversation. I thought, better she than me.

"I wish we could get a picture of the sheep in the field," Stella said. "They look so 'Irish'. And look there is purple and pink heather."

"The heather is Irish. We have sheep in America," I teased. "I want pictures of the old, old cemeteries."

"You're weird."

"I know. All mystery writers are weird. Didn't you know?"

"I didn't know that until I met you."

McKinnon must have read my mind because he stood up in front of the bus and said, "Our next stop is Glendalough, where we find ruins of St. Kevin's monastic settlement. Glendalough means Glen of Two Lakes."

St. Kevin was a hermit priest who built a monastic settlement in the 6th century. His Irish name means 'gentle one'. The settlement became the center of learning throughout Europe. The round tower remains as well as some buildings from the 8th and 12th century."

We exited the bus and walked up a slight rise. Stella shivered in the brisk wind. Looking back for the bus she said, "I should have brought my windbreaker." It is colder here than I expected."

"Rory has already moved the bus," I teased. "I'm sure he is somewhere drinking hot coffee."

She gave me a disgusted look. "I don't care what Rory is drinking or where. I just wanted my jacket, I'm cold."

"Take my windbreaker. I'm not using it. My shirt is heavy and I have another under it." I gave her my navy blue jacket with the hood.

My first view of the round tower was heart stopping. Nothing in my experience prepared me for the feeling of ancient history come to life. How many ancient people had trod this path, lived and was buried in the cemetery?

Stella and I meandered with the group to gape

up at the round tower and take pictures. Then we scattered to various other picture points. I was fascinated with the crumbling tombstones and I tried in vain to read the inscriptions. The Celtic cross was prominent on many of them.

The perfectly preserved chapel and the small building said to belong to the monk St. Kevin was beautifully set in green grass against a wooded hill. Other ruins were scattered through the cemetery, built with stones placed there by human hands many years ago. I knew I would write about this place sometime soon.

I tried to imagine what this place would have looked like with workshops, guesthouses, farm buildings, dwellings for monks and I could not see it as it was then. Graveyards were the most sacred place in a Celtic Monastery. They were always located within the walls of the monastery.

I looked around to ask Stella to take a picture of me in front of the ruined chapel, but I couldn't see her. In fact, I seemed to have wandered away from the tour crowd. Remembering my experience of the night before, I hurried through the dim paths to find people. Anyone would do. I just didn't want to be alone in this place.

A group was listening to McKinnon tell that the pink bleeding heart vine that seemingly grew wild was sometimes called Mother Mary's Tears. Stella wasn't in the group. I couldn't see her anywhere. My navy blue windbreaker would stand out among the others, wouldn't it?

Logan and April came up behind me. She didn't waste any time, I thought, then chided myself for the feeling.

"I can't find Stella," I blurted. We were wandering among the ruins and we were separated. Do you see her? She has to be here."

"We haven't seen her," April volunteered. "But then we were kind of busy with other things."

As the group moved toward the exit, I became more agitated. "I must find her. Maybe she's lost and can't find her way out of the maze of paths and stones."

"We'll find her." Logan removed April's hand from his arm. "What is she wearing?"

"She borrowed my navy blue windbreaker and she is wearing jeans and sneakers."

"Hey, McKinnon," Logan called. "Has anyone seen Ms. Gerritson? She seems to have wandered off." Several people shook their heads no.

"We'll help you look." Matt and Monica came toward us. "She's probably nearby, engrossed in taking pictures. Where did you see her last?"

I indicated the area where Stella and I were taking pictures of the chapel ruins. We scattered and began calling her name. I was grateful that Logan kept me in sight. I didn't want to be alone among the ruins.

Venturing off the beaten path, I noticed the grass was flattened as if someone had passed that way. Then I saw the Tootsie Roll wrapper.

"Look, Logan. Someone came this way and dropped a Tootsie Roll wrapper. Stella must have come this way."

"And you had Tootsie Rolls in the pocket of your windbreaker?"

"Tootsie Rolls and wrappers too. I don't drop them on the ground. I put them in my pocket until I . . ."

"There is another one," he said. We began following the Tootsie Roll wappers through the tangled undergrowth.

"Why would she come this way?" I wondered aloud.

"I don't think she came of her own accord. This looks like more than one person came this way," Logan commented increasing his speed.

I began to shake from fear. "The man last night?"

"Could be," was his terse answer.

We rounded the corner of a particularly large memorial and there she was, slumped against the stone. She was unconscious.

I ran to her. "Stella. Stella. Help me," I implored Logan.

"Don't move her." His voice was sharp. She's injured. He raised his voice, "We've found her over here." The other searchers joined us.

"What happened?"

"She's hurt."

Their comments were a jumble as I ignored Logan's command and gathered Stella into my arms. She roused, protesting against my embrace.

"Thank God, you found me." She tried to rise but I held her firmly.

"Stella what happened to you?"

She brushed the hood of the windbreaker back from her face with a shaking hand. "He hit me."

Logan took over, pushing me out of the way.

"Who hit you?"

"The man. He grabbed me. I was taking pictures and didn't see him. He pushed and dragged me here. I dropped the Tootsie Roll wrappers. Did you see them?

"Yes, we saw them. That is how we found you."

"Oh, honey. I'm so relieved to find you. Thankfully, you had the presence of mind to drop the wrappers. We would never have found you without them."

She struggled to rise. Logan and Matt on each side of her. "He wanted something. He kept saying, 'Give it to me.' When he heard you call, he hit me and ran away."

"Don't say anything more," Logan ordered with a stern look at me.

"Nothing more about it Stella, it was a mistake. Can you walk to the bus?"

"Yes, the hood on the jacket took most of the blow. I'm ok. I think," her laugh was shaky.

Matt and Monica held her arms as she walked slowly toward the bus. Logan stayed behind, studying the ground.

"You think it was the same man, don't you? The man from last night?" I said.

"Yes, I do. She was wearing your jacket. He thought he was taking you. Ms. James, you must be careful. These people are terrorists. They will not be gentle if they do not find the microchip. Please keep our conversation last night a secret. We can't afford to cause a panic."

We were nearly to the bus. I noticed Rory ran

half way up the path to get to Stella. She has certainly made a conquest, I thought. That is good. If he sticks close to her, maybe she'll be safe. And who is going to keep you safe, Lacey? You're the one they want.

Chapter 7

We got Stella settled in the coach. Neither of us heard a word of McKinnon's speech as we rolled along County Wicklow. I held her hand and worried as she leaned her head against the back of the seat with her eyes closed

The next stop was Avoca to tour the weaving mill. Before we scattered, McKinnon told us Avoca Handweavers was the oldest, surviving, working woolen mill in Ireland. Avoca was also known as Ballykissangel. First located on the banks of the fast flowing River Avoca in 1723, it was a corn grinding as well as a spinning and weaving mill.

Several people on the tour immediately went to the gift shop. Others went to the weaving house, situated up a path bordered with colorful flowers.

I found a handy stone wall in the sun, near the bus, for Stella to sit while I ran into the gift shop for a cup of tea. She had a knot the size of a golf ball where the assailant hit her and she had a terrific headache. She agreed to take an aspirin with her tea.

Everyone was curious about what happened to Stella. But Logan had cautioned us to soft pedal the incident. Maureen wouldn't let it go.

"What in the world was she doing wandering off away from the group?" She bellowed.

"She likes to take pictures. She's very good and has had several framed for sale. She was looking for something unusual." I hoped I curtailed Maureen's questions.

Rory stayed with Stella while Alice walked with me as we toured the mill where articles are woven both by machine and by hand. "I hope she is okay," Alice said in her quiet way.

"She'll be fine. Just a little rest, I'm sure." I liked this quiet little woman, who traveled the world alone.

Alice and I bought a few small things in the gift shop and had them shipped home, in deference to McKinnon's request.

McKinnon herded us back into the bus with a promise to stop at the *Dunbrody*. The replica of the ships that took 2 million emigrants to North America were called 'coffin ships' because so many people died on the crossing. Not having time for a tour of the boat, we had to be content to view it from the dock. I decided if it were up to me to cross the ocean in that small sailboat, my family would still be in Ireland. I couldn't imagine putting my whole family and few possessions on one of the boats and sailing thousands of miles to an unknown continent.

The tall masts and sails of the *Dunbrody* set my writer's imagination working. I wished again for my laptop. What was I thinking? I'm on vacation. But a writer's imagine never stops. Work reminded me that I needed to look at the galleys of my latest book. A.P. insisted I bring them and expected them as soon as I returned.

I took pictures and made notes about the replica. The *Dunbrody* is a recreation of the coffin ship in which John F. Kennedy's grandfather traveled to America.

We left the *Dunbrody* behind and settled in to the bus for the next stop. McKinnon told us Waterford is the fifth largest city in Ireland, settled in 914 by Vikings, making it the oldest city in Ireland.

Stella's headache was better, but our hotel room was welcome. "Our luggage isn't up yet, but we can rest awhile before we go out again," I said, as Stella stretched out on the pristine bed.

"Oh, yuck," I said, as I peered out the open window. "This view sucks and stinks too."

"What is it?" Stella wasn't interested enough to get up and look.

"It is a muddy ditch and there is debris in it."

Stella chuckled. "We are near the ocean. When the tide comes in, water

will fill up your muddy ditch and it will be pretty again and probably not smell bad either. McKinnon told us the Port of Waterford is the closest major port to mainland England. He mentioned a walking tour of the old part of town beginning in about thirty minutes. I think a walk will clear my head. Are you up for it?"

"I'm tired but I'll go with you. Can't miss a chance to see something I'll never see again. Grab your jacket, this time."

"Got it. I'll never wear your jacket again. It gained me a bump on my head. Someone thought I was you."

"Let's don't think about that, okay? I get the shakes just thinking that man could have killed you. Where's my notebook?"

"Right where you keep it. In your carry bag. Don't try to change the subject. Get your camera."

It was more of a run than a walk through the city. The guide raced through what he called the Viking Triangle, consisting of narrow streets and medieval architecture. The most interesting was Reginald's Tower. He hardly gave us time to take pictures. Wanting to take advantage of the historical views of the oldest City in Ireland, we fell behind the tour group. It was beginning to get dusky dark and the buildings seemed to close in around us as we walked faster to catch up.

"Did they go this way?" I asked.

"I don't know. I was trying to get a picture of the tower," Stella said, looking around. "Oh look. There is Logan."

"Thanks for waiting for us," I said, when we caught up with him.

"Are you both complete idiots?" he asked. "Someone wants something you have and is willing to do anything to get it and you stall around this place alone. You should have your heads examined.

"We are not complete idiots," I defended.

"We've never had terrorists after us before. Besides, that guide is walking too fast."

"Everyone else is able to keep up."

We strode along in silence for awhile before he said, "I'm sorry. I'm concerned about your safety."

CHAPTER 8

Logan and I were silent as we finished the tour. Stella kept her eyes straight ahead. It was less than an hour until the dinner hour when we returned to the hotel.

Stella was annoyed "Our bags still aren't here. I really wanted to change before dinner."

"They should be here by now. It's been a couple of hours since we arrived. What could have happened to them? I'm sure they were in the bus. I saw Rory stow them myself."

"We need to contact McKinnon. He needs to know there is a mix-up with the luggage." I reached for the telephone. I finally located McKinnon in the bar. He was apologetic and promised to find the luggage ASAP.

Stella and I contented ourselves with freshening ourselves with what we had available which wasn't much in the way of makeup.

Personally, I felt sticky and dirty after a day on the road.

McKinnon met us at the door of the dining room. He apologized again. "I haven't found your luggage, yet. I'm sorry. It is unusual for two bags to go missing. I have the hotel staff searching for them. Rory remembers loading the bags, so the problem is here. We'll gi' your luggage, never fear." He had lapsed into his Irish brogue again.

Dinner was a quiet affair. We sat at a table with Alice Baker and the Page couple. The food was excellent. As always, Salmon and beef were on the menu, along with two kinds of potatoes and other vegetables. Our group was congenial but all of us were too tired to converse much. I noticed Logan and April sat at an intimate table for two. He saw me staring and winked at me. The Fletchers, Hancocks, the Edingtons and the Kings occupied a long table in the center of the room. The wine was flowing and they all seemed to be in better spirits than me. The only chatter seemed to be Maureen mourning the fact that the Waterford Crystal Factory had recently closed. Several people soothed her by telling her the beautiful crystal was still available in several area stores.

Shortly before dessert was served, McKinnon informed us our baggage was found in an empty room in the hotel. "I cannot imagine how this happened, and I am profoundly sorry. Your luggage is in your room now."

"Thank you. I'm sure it was just a mix up and won't happen again." I just wanted to forget the whole mess and go to my room.

Sure enough, the bags were in our room. We were unpacking night things, when we heard a knock on the door.

Logan had raised his fist for another knock when Stella opened the door. "Don't unpack anything else until I look at your luggage," he ordered. "A hotel staffer was paid to put your bags in an empty room. No doubt, someone searched them. I doubt anything was put into your suitcases, but we can't be too sure."

"You two stand over here, while I examine your luggage."

"Now, just a minute." I was angry. "We have gone through too much with this intrigue. I was flattened in the airport and assaulted at the dinner theatre. Stella was knocked unconscious at the cemetery and now you say our luggage may contain explosives."

"Look, I didn't start this. Enemies of our country do not care how many people they hurt or even kill." Logan's eyes blazed with fury. "You have to realize that. I'm sure your luggage doesn't contain explosives, but perhaps they left a clue. I need to look, so stand back."

I backed down real quick when he put it that way. "I hope they took the galleys," I muttered.

"What?"

"Nothing." I sank into a convenient chair and watched Logan look through my jeans, shirts and unmentionables. At least, he was looking through Stella's too. The hated galleys were still there, and I still had to proof them. Even if terrorists took over Ireland and half of America, A.P. would expect those galleys proofed when I got home.

Logan pronounced our luggage safe and left without an apology. I slammed the door behind him. Stella grinned. "Did that help any?"

"No." Then I laughed.

Later, I tackled the galleys while Stella lounged on the bed, writing in her journal.

"I've had enough of this." I stood up and stretched. "I'd like a cup of tea. How about you? There is an urn on the first floor. I noticed they have tea and coffee as well as cookies. Can I get you a cup of something?"

"Sure. Make it a cup of tea. No cookies for me but no doubt you have your eye on a sweet of some kind. You know, Logan is probably standing outside the door waiting for you to escape." She grinned.

I made a face at her and grabbed my room card. "I'll go down the stairs. He'll be watching the elevator," I teased. We were on the third floor and the taking the stairs seemed like a good idea. Riding in the bus all day made the old lady arthritis rear its ugly head.

On the second floor landing, I literally ran into Craig Cranfield and Carolyn Vaughn. They jumped apart guiltily. There was definitely more going on than conversation.

"Sorry," I mumbled and went on downstairs. How would I face them and their spouses in the morning?

CHAPTER 9

I talked to myself all night. Carolyn and Craig are not your business. Leave it alone. You are a nosy old fuddy-duddy. Forget about it. I knew when the tide came in. I heard the sounds of the early morning boats. I heard every move Stella made. I felt tired and grumpy when Stella opened the window and let in the cold salt-tinged air.

"Shut the window. It's cold." I buried my head under the covers.

"Wake up. It's going to be a beautiful day." She stretched and luxuriated in the cool air. "We are in Ireland and today we visit a castle."

"You sure don't sound like someone who got conked on the head yesterday."

"I feel fine. Now get up. I'm hungry. I'm going to shower and when I get finished I'd better find your behind up and eager to get on with the day." She grabbed her robe and gave me what was intended to be a ferocious look.

I laughed and sank down into the warm bed for a quick snooze. I knew Stella and I knew she would be in the shower for at least a half-hour. What she did for half an hour is beyond me. It takes me about five minutes in the shower. On second thought, maybe I should borrow some of her lotions and crèmes. April was getting a little too feisty for my comfort. Logan was a good-looking man and he was here to protect me, after all.

Stella was dressed when I left the bathroom. She looked good in a pin-stripe pants suit and loafers. Was Rory the reason she decided to dress up?

"Did you remember we have to have the bags out by seven. We are moving on today?" Stella was zipping up her suitcase.

"Oh shoot! I forgot about that. This will just take a minute. Help me, will you?" I grabbed a few things and stuffed them into my suitcase. "Not that. I intend to wear that. Fold this and put the scarf in the carry bag. Thanks for the help." We dragged the bags into the hall.

"I'm almost afraid to let them out of my sight." I slipped the room card into my pocket. "Let's go to breakfast, then return for the carry bags and jackets."

I poked at my hair and admired the image of myself in the elevator mirror. Not bad. My windbreaker would go with the grey slacks and matching striped top. One would think we were two old ladies on the prowl for rich husbands. Wonder what a Homeland Security agent makes a year? I smiled to myself and patted my pockets for Tootsie Rolls.

Alice stepped on the elevator at the next floor down. She was cheerful, asking about Stella's head and commenting on the wonderful weather. We walked to the dining room chatting where we found complete chaos.

The Edingtons and Kings were seated at a table for four. Their breakfast was untouched as Maureen stood over the table screeching, "Which of you bitches stole my ring?"

The old couples cringed under the barrage. Hadley stood up. "Look here, Maureen. What is this about?"

"About, about," Maureen was out of control. "It's about my missing ring. Where is it? Who took it?"

"I assure you madam none of us took your ring." Curtis was more polite than I would have been. AnnaLise looked near tears and Rose continued to drink her tea as if nothing was happening around her. Hadley's face was pale as he placed a protective hand on Rose's shoulder.

I looked around for McKinnon. As usual, he wasn't around. Surely he wasn't in the bar this early. I motioned to Matt Page who was just entering the dining room with Monica. He rushed over and took Maureen by the arm. She angrily brushed him away. She was so mad I expected to see steam coming out of her nose.

"Maureen, calm down. What is wrong?" Matt patiently tried to draw the irate woman away from the older couple's table.

"Someone stole my ring." Maureen huffed. "Vern bought it for me at a little shop in Waterford last evening. I showed it to these people when they were in our suite for drinks. Now it's gone. They stole it. It is very valuable. Vernon doesn't buy cheap things." She rambled on and on.

"I stepped close to AnnaLise when I saw she was trembling. Billie Owensby came running, patting and cooing to AnnaLise. I stepped away to hear Matt say, "Where is Vernon? We need to look in your room. I"m sure your ring is there."

"Vern went out for a paper. I don't know where he went. He's around here somewhere. But my ring is gone. One of them took it. I know it. We invited the four of them along with Andy and Jo to our room last night for a nightcap. Andy and Jo are longtime friends. They wouldn't steal from me." Maureen seemed to be calming down.

Matt took her arm, "Let's look in your room again." He led her out of the room.

AnnaLise stood on shaky legs as Billie took her arm and led her out of the dining room also. Stella and I were silent as we helped ourselves to the food buffet, then joined Alice at a table for four.

"Oh my, that woman," was Alice's refined comment. "I never saw anyone make such a fuss."

"I hope they find the darned thing. If they don't we'll never hear the end of it. She'll probably find it under something." I helped myself to hot water to weaken the strong coffee.

"Is anyone excited about the castle we'll be visiting today?" Irene Brouchard said, stopping by our table with her empty tray. "McKinnon has brochures in the coach. It is a popular tourist site. We leave in 15 minutes."

"I've read about it in the tourist guide. It is a beautiful castle," Alice said. "I think we are ready to go to the room and then to the bus."

Later, as we boarded the bus, I managed to whisper to Matt, "Did you find the ring?"

"No, her bags had been picked up. We searched the room. I think when she unpacks she will find the ring."

As usual, Maureen and Vernon captured the front seat of the bus with their pals, Andy and Jo Fletcher across from them on the other front seat.

"Might be nice to sit on the front seat occasionally," I murmured to Stella as we sank into seats further back. Like a little pup, Logan stayed close behind us.

"Shhh." Stella dropped her head below the seat back. "I don't want her screeching at us."

McKinnon took center stage, his back to the road, facing his audience. Bracing himself, he began to tell us the day's tour. "We will backtrack a bit to Kilkenny to view the fabulous Kilkenny Castle. The Castle is a popular tourist attraction because it has been completely restored. The Castle was built in the 12th century on the banks of the River Nore. It was the principal seat of the Butler family for a number of years. Many original furnishings were sold over the years, but those have been located and returned to the castle, so you can experience the lifestyle of the family.

"The first castle was square shaped with four towers. Three of those original towers remain. A guide will take you through the castle. No cameras are allowed inside, but the beautiful park around it offers many opportunities for pictures. You will see the servant's stairs and remember to notice the family burial plot where the family dog's tombstone is more ornate that those of the family. Meanwhile, enjoy the roadside views while Rory entertains us with a song. You didn't know Rory could drive and sing at the same time, did you? Well, Rory and I are Irishmen and all Irishmen drink Guinness and sing."

I was surprised when Rory began to sing in a rich tenor. He sang several Irish favorites and then segued into *My Wild Irish Rose."*

I caught him looking in the rear view mirror at Stella as he sang. I elbowed her. "He is singing to you. Stella."

"Stop it. He is not singing to me." Her face flushed rosy pink and she dropped her eyes to her hands.

Kilkenny Castle was all McKinnon promised. Built in an enormous U shaped, the grey stone edifice was breathtaking in its beauty, a true picture of Irish history. Immense gardens in front and back added to the beauty. Stella and I immediately began to take pictures, but McKinnon hurried the group along so he could pay the fee for us to tour the castle. Irene Bouchard joined the group, pleading she had never seen the castle and if she were leading a tour she must know about the sights available.

Wandering about in the great cavernous rooms, my imagination took control and I wondered what it was like to live here in the past. The rooms were huge with high ceilings and many doors and windows.

My writer's mind got the best of me. "Imagine ladies in beautiful long dresses sitting in the brocade chairs, embroidering while a lute player entertained them." I was in another world but Irene brought me down quick.

"They would be hunkered around the fireplace, dressed in many layers trying to keep warm."

Oh well, to each his own. I preferred my dream to hers. Mitch Logan stayed close to Stella and me. April stayed close to him. I felt like I was being followed and deliberately tried to elude the two. At one point, he managed to get close enough to me to whisper. "Stop trying to be a hero. You are still in danger and this is perfect place for an attack."

April gave me a dirty look and I gave Logan a dirty look. I even conjured up a story of a beautiful princess locked in the castle. The wicked witch looked like April and her mother looked like Irene Bouchard. Logan was not Prince Charming.

After the long walking tour of the castle, it was pleasant to sit in the garden and enjoy the array of varied colored flowers. Alice named many of the flowers but I was content just to enjoy their beauty. Stella, of course, took many close ups as well as landscaped shots. No doubt, some of her castle pictures would end up framed.

The sun was bright enough to ward off the slight chill of the day. The river was over the rise and the sound of flowing water was peaceful. We stayed there for a time before boarding the bus to traveling down to Cork.

There were many picturesque places but the bus did not stop for pictures. I made a mental wish list to return at leisure to explore the countryside.

CHAPTER 10

"You know the legend of the Blarney Stone. Kissing the Blarney Stone endows the kisser with a gift of gab and a skill at flattery. A visit to Ireland would not be complete with a visit to kiss the Blarney Stone." McKinnon lectured as the bus rumbled down the road.

Rory reached for the microphone, one hand on the steering wheel and his eyes still on the road, he declared, "No doubt, our esteemed tour guide has kissed the Blarney Stone."

McKinnon smiled at the teasing. "I have not kissed the Blarney stone. I would not put these pure lips where millions of others have slobbered," he declared.

"The stone is located at the top of Blarney Castle. The castle was first built in the 11th century of wood, then stone. The stone structure was destroyed but rebuilt in 1446 by one of Ireland's greatest Chieftains, Cormac McCarthy. There are many legends about the Blarney Stone, the most likely one being it was given to McCarthy by Robert the Bruce in 1314. When the castle was rebuilt the stone became part of the new castle. The castle is in ruins but Blarney House is open to the public. Gardeners worldwide visit the surrounding gardens. Within the gardens, you'll find rock formations with fanciful names such as Druid Circle, Witches Cave and Wishing Steps.

"To kiss the Blarney Stone, a visitor must first climb to the peak of the castle, lean over the edge of the parapet backwards. It is necessary that an assistant hold your legs to keep you from falling to your death as depicted in recent movies.

"We will stop here long enough for you to climb to the top of the castle and kiss the Blarney Stone if you wish. Although the grounds are beautiful, we do not have time to linger."

"Do you have a great desire to kiss the Blarney Stone?" Stella was gathering her camera in preparation to exiting the bus.

"Not really. How about you?" I stood up and stretched as bones popped and cracked.

"I'm not sure these old legs will climb that far and I certainly have no desire to bend over backwards over a stone parapet while someone holds my legs."

Rory must have overheard us. "Ladies, I assure you the climb is long and kissing the stone is not a comfortable position. May I tempt you to join me for a drink while we wait?"

Logan pulled me aside as Stella walked away

with Rory. "I ask you to consider not climbing to the castle. It is a tough climb and many areas that could be dangerous if you are not aware of those around you."

I raised an eyebrow. "I'm sure April would not pass an opportunity to accompany you to the highest peak and allow you to hold her legs as she kisses the Blarney Stone."

I think he muttered a dirty word. "I can't get rid of her. She's like a buzzing mosquito. I brush her away and in a minute she is back."

I was surprised that several of the tour group decided to climb the hill to Blarney Castle. It was a tour for seniors after all. The rest of us found a bench in the shade, with a view of the castle, to remind us of our infirmities.

Rory was a treasure trove of Irish History. Several of us took notes as he entertained us with a rich Irish brogue.

Billie Owensby buzzed around Hadley and AnnaLise. A.P. should have hired to her to look after her aunt. I was ashamed of my thoughts because I hadn't done much to earn my trip to Ireland. I was having entirely too much stress without bothering with the old couple.

Rory asked Stella about the Ozarks. I was surprised to see her open up and talk about our homeland. "I have traveled to several places in the world, but I always return to the Ozarks. They are beautiful and residents are never bored because the seasons change giving us new experiences and views. I wish I could show you some of my pictures of the Ozarks." I don't think I've ever heard her talk so much to strangers.

"Stella takes wonderful pictures. Many have been on magazine covers." I smiled at my friend who was opening up to these strangers and having a good time.

"Any magazines we might have seen?" Rory was certainly interested in Stella. I hope he isn't married. He isn't wearing a wedding ring so perhaps it is okay..

"Nothing that would be published here." Stella was being modest. "I could send you a sample of my photography when I get home or if you have internet, some of my pictures are on my web page. Stella was speaking directly to Rory. I felt like a third wheel.

Not to be ignored, Irene Bouchard spoke up. "You two Missouri girls are talented. Lacey writes books and Stella takes pictures." Did I detect a slight sneer?

"What is your latest book, Lacey? I'll look for it when I get back home." Alice had her pen and notebook ready to take down my answer.

Now it was my turn to be modest. "*Murder in the Ozarks*" came out in January. I also write historical romance. I'm getting a lot of material here in Ireland. I'm thinking my next book will be set here in Ireland."

"Will it be a murder mystery?" This from AnnaLise.

I don't know. With all the history in Ireland, I will probably write a historical."

"Why do you write about murder? I don't even like to think about it." Curtis picked up Rose's scarf and put it around her shoulders.

I write cozy mysteries. Just simple little stories about murder, theft, kidnapping. I guess I like the puzzle of a mystery. One thing about mysteries is the good guys always win. Would anyone like a Tootsie Roll?" I passed around a handful.

We spent a pleasant hour chatting, roaming around, taking pictures and relaxing.

All too soon, McKinnon was shepherding us into the bus for the five-mile drive to Cork. From there we would go to Cobh (pronounced Cove) to tour the Cobh Heritage Museum.

Our destination was the museum that is located in the Old Railway Hall. Stella and I wandered through, commenting on the period furniture and life-size figures depicting the life of the Irish during different times of the emigration.

"There are a million stories here." I lingered over the figures of a mother and four children, all their belongings in one carpetbag.

"And you can write their stories, when we get home. This trip is your inspiration and the internet your source."

I smiled at Stella. Although not a writer, she is a great encourager.

Irene Bouchard was standing nearby, sounding like a tour guide. Today her long red hair was caught up under a green hat that matched her suit. "The statue on the harbour is of Annie Moore and her brothers. Annie was the first person to be admitted to the U.S. through Ellis Island, Jan. 1, 1892."

Ah, Annie could be my heroine. I could write

about her life in Ireland, then in America. I made scribbled notes before I forgot my idea.

"Two and a half million Irish people sailed from Cobh Harbour to make a new life in America." Irene was reading from the same brochure I held in my hand. Our group listened with interest. "Cobh Harbour was the major embarkation for men, women and children sent to penal colonies in New Zealand or Australia."

Another idea, if not a book, then a historical piece, maybe for children. My mind was running in high gear.

"I need a cold drink and a snack. Would you like something? I asked Stella.

"Water would be nice. I'll meet you down by the water.

I went over to the snack bar and ordered two waters and a candy bar. Turning around with my snacks, I noticed Rose and Curtis at a table nearby. Curtis was clearing the table of sandwich papers. Rose was putting a saltshaker in her purse. I stopped dead in my tracks. A saltshaker! Surely not!

Then she put her purse on the table while she put on her jacket. Curtis quickly rescued the saltshaker and put it on another table.

I met Stella near a navy boat anchored there. She read from one of the brochures we had picked up. Cobh Harbour is one of the world's natural deepwater harbours." Cobh is a popular stop for cruise ships.

We viewed an Irish Navy ship that was in port. McKinnon was standing nearby talking with one of the seamen. "This beautiful craft is one of only eleven ships in the Irish Navy. Their current duties are patrolling the harbour and surrounding coastal waters for drug runners," he told us.

"Cobh Harbour holds the distinction of being the last port of call for the ill-fated Titanic." McKinnon was in fine lecture form and we crowded around to hear. "More than one hundred passengers of the Lusitanian are buried in Old Church Cemetery. The Lusitanian was sunk by a German U boat in 1915. Bodies were buried as they washed up on the shore."

"Any chance for a visit to the Old Church Cemetery?" I asked.

"It would be an interesting stop, but we really must be on our way to reach our hotel for a late dinner." He acted genuinely sorry.

After another long ride, the bus stopped in a small village for a bathroom break. We tumbled from the bus to take pictures of castle ruins not far away. Then we scrambled across the street to a little store to buy gum, candy and water. The bathrooms were on the third floor, so we took turns ascending and descending the narrow stairs.

Stella and I waited to cross the street to board the bus, still gawking at the castle and wishing we had time to explore. We had gained the opposite side of the street when we heard shouts and tires screeching.

"Stella, its Hadley and AnnaLise. That car nearly hit them."

Stella was already running across the street along with several others from the tour. Billie Owensby reached the old couple first, being on the side of the street where they started. They were unhurt but shaken. AnnaLise had fallen down and skinned her knees. She pushed Billie away and reached for Stella. Stella lifted the frail old woman to her feet and hugged her. Annalise's head fell to Stella's shoulder and she rested there.

"I'll call an ambulance." McKinnon was already dialing his cell phone.

"Don't do that." Hadley ordered. Give Annie some water. She'll be fine, won't you darlin'?" He was obviously shaken. He reached for AnnaLise. "She's my sweetheart. I'll take care of her. Willing hands helped the old couple across the street and into the bus. Stella took Annalise to the back of the bus for privacy and cleaned her knees and legs, bandaging them from the first aid kit on the bus.

"You will be sore tomorrow. Try to take a warm bath tonight to help the soreness," Stella advised.

"Thanks honey." Hadley was anxious to push Stella away. "We'll be fine. I'll take care of her." He put an arm around AnnaLise protectively.

Chapter 11

Our next stop was the luxurious Muckross Park Hotel. It sprawled across several acres of land with beautiful trees and grass. The main edifice resembled a castle or ancient manor house.

Stella gathered our scattered bits and pieces as in preparation for disembarking as the bus stopped near the annex where our rooms were located. McKinnon gave us room numbers as we exited the bus. We were surprised to see that our room was on the first floor while Hadley and Analise had a second floor room. It didn't make sense for them to climb the stairs to their room, when we able bodied were allowed first floor access. McKinnon promised to look into it.

Alice's room was next to ours and when she opened the door, she discovered she was in a suite. Our room, Stella's and mine was one room. It was luxurious, but again it didn't make sense that Alice who traveled alone ended up with a suite while couples only had one room.

Maureen raised a fuss as usual, complaining loudly that it was unfair. She and Vernon should have the suite and she demanded it be changed immediately.

Alice graciously offered to change with them, but McKinnon promised to sort it out and get back to us.

As soon as we were in our room, Stella locked the door and motioned me to the bed where she had sat down. "I have to tell you what AnnaLise said to me."

"She said something to you after she fell?"

"When I picked her up and hugged her she murmured, 'Pushed me.' I was so shocked, I couldn't think for a minute. Then I decided to let it pass for the moment."

"Who could have pushed her? Who was on that side of the street?" Can you remember? Questions came to me thick and fast.

"Do you think someone pushed her or did she just fall?" Stella wasn't willing to point a finger at anyone.

AnnaLise was my responsibility on this trip although I was doing a poor job of being a bodyguard. "I think it is possible. A.P. thought she made a mistake when she married Hadley. They were so worried they planned to come on this trip to protect her."

"Right." Stella slowly nodded her head. "Who was on that side of the street before AnnaLise fell?"

"Curtis could have done it, although he was in

danger too when he stopped to pick her up. The school teachers were over there and Billie Owensby, Logan and April, too." I had to stop and smile at his description of April as a mosquito. She was living up to the name, clutching him every time he moved.

"I don't think Logan is here to worry about AnnaLise and Hadley. The schoolteachers are a possibility, but I can't think why they would harm an old lady. I don't think April has enough sense to be a danger to anyone except Logan." I smiled again. "Logan referred to April and a persistent mosquito. I thought it an apt description."

Stella laughed outright. "It is a good description and I'm sure she is a detriment to Logan's true reason for being here."

"Maybe we should make a suspect list. What about Irene Bouchard? Where was she when AnnaLise was pushed? Matt and Monica entered the bus just ahead of us so they are not suspect. Alice was with us." My head was beginning to spin with the possibilities.

"Irene was talking with Rory in front of the bus, so she didn't push AnnaLise." Stella was firm in her knowledge of where Irene was.

"Oh, you keep track of Irene and Rory, do you?" I teased.

Stella blushed. "Stop it!"

"I'm sorry. I just think it is neat that you have captured the attentions of a man on this trip."

"He and McKinnon probably choose a woman on each tour for special attention. It is good for business." Stella ignored me and began to unpack her suitcase.

I leaned close to her. "But he sings *Wild Irish Rose* to you."

She gave me a disgusted look and retreated to the bathroom.

I laid out my own outfit for the evening. It was to be dress up kind of dinner, so I resorted to my old reliable black pants, paired with a white sweater.

When Stella came out of the bathroom, I was ready to go in but stopped long enough to comment. "You know, I've noticed Billie Owensby is always hovering around AnnaLise. I'm going to call A.P. and see if she knows anything about her. I wonder if I should share all this with Logan. I don't think it has anything to do with our problem, but he should be aware of what is going on. Something else I need to tell you and him, the other night when I went out for tea I ran into Craig and Carolyn being lovey-dovey in the stairway."

Stella was shocked. "You're kidding. They seem like such a wholesome foursome."

"I'm thinking I should tell Logan. We don't know what an extremist looks like. They could be lying through their teeth."

Stella chose to wear the outfit she wore on our second evening in Dublin. As she pulled the Squash Blossom Necklace over her head, I had an idea. "Let's set Billie Owensby up. She says she is from Sedona. Tonight I will comment on your necklace. You say you bought it in Sedona but make up a store. Then we'll ask Billie if she knows the store. If she says yes, we'll know she is lying."

We met Alice in the hall ready for dinner. She

was climbing the stairs. "I want to knock on Hadley and Annalisa's door. I feel bad because I got a ground floor room and they didn't."

"I'm sure McKinnon will straighten everything out. If he doesn't Maureen will have his head. But you deserve a ground floor room too." I patted her shoulder. She was such a sweet person. "We should check on Annalisa's condition after her fall. Do you mind if we go with you?"

"Not at all, then we can go to dinner. I'm happy for the company." We climbed the stairs and Alice knocked on the door. Hadley answered her knock.

"How is AnnaLise doing? Stella took the lead.

"She is sleeping. I gave her a sleeping pill. She took a hot bath and hopefully, she will feel better in the morning."

"Are you coming out to dinner?" Alice inquired.

"No, I'll have something sent over. Thank you for your concern." He sounded tired and defeated.

We walked across the courtyard to dinner. I spotted Logan talking with the concierge and for once April was not with him. "You guys go on into dinner," I told Stella and Alice. "I need to speak to Logan a minute."

I quickly filled him in on AnnaLise's accusation and Craig and Carolyn's indiscretions.

"I doubt AnnaLise and Hadley have anything to do with our problem, since you were sent by AnnaLise's niece to protect her." He lounged against the wall to the dining room, looking both ways.

"Keeping an eye out for April?" I couldn't help

teasing him.

He ignored my jibe. "I'll look into the schoolteachers' past. My office has checked the background on most of the people on the tour. I'll make a call to be sure we didn't miss anything."

"You've check my background?" My upraised eyebrows caused him to laugh.

"You betcha. I know the name of your first boyfriend."

"You're kidding."

"Nope. We had to be sure you weren't part of a plot to transfer the microchip to another agent."

"And you found out I'm clean?"

"Clean as the driven snow."

"And just as boring."

"I didn't say that."

He put his hand on my back and we strolled into dinner.

We joined Stella and Alice at a large table. Billie Owensby and Irene Bouchard sat across from them. April came in late dressed in a stunning halter-top dress with a dreamy, swishy skirt. She didn't conceal her disappointment that Logan's table was full and she had to sit with the Fletchers and Hancocks.

The waiter hovered. "You have choice of grilled salmon or beef, Two kinds of potatoes and steamed vegetables. Desert is crème Brule. I will take your entrée order now."

Typically, I chose beef and Stella salmon. The girl was going to turn into a fish before the trip was over. But then, I guess that was preferable to a cow. I choked back a chuckle and Logan looked at me with an uplifted eyebrow.

While we waited for the first course, I leaned over to Stella and said, "Stella, that is beautiful necklace. Where did you get it again?"

Stella was ready for my question. "I got it in Sedona, Arizona. My daughter and I were visiting there. We found this little shop on one of the main streets, Sylvia's. There were so much beautiful jewelry, I couldn't decide which to get."

"Billie, you are from Sedona. Do you know Sylvia's?"

"Of course, anyone who has been to Sedona knows Sylvia's." Billie's answer was curt before turning her attention to her appetizer.

Stella looked at me with her mouth open. I made a quick close your mouth motion to her.

After a scrumptious dinner, it was pleasant to walk in the gardens. The hotel seemed to be full and many people were taking advantage of the walkways. All the flowers in Ireland are glorious, probably because of the mild winters and moist environment. Alice was knowledgeable about the flora and fauna and finally confessed to being an avid gardener.

It had been a long day, and by dusky dark we were ready to relax in the gorgeous room. McKinnon had not made provisions for any of us to move, so we felt comfortable in unpacking, as we were to stay here for three nights. What a relief to spread out and not have to worry about early morning packing.

Stella earnestly wrote postcards and I reluctantly picked up the galleys. After a while, feeling restricted, I changed into my pink granny gown and was more comfortable. Before long, yawns overtook me, and I went to bed. I'm not sure when Stella went to bed but I know we were both sleeping when we heard noises outside our door.

We jumped up perplexed and cautiously peeked out the door. Our room was at the foot of the stairway and the end of the hall leading outside. The noise continued and accelerated into a distinct "help me, help me."

Alarmed, we looked up to see Hadley clutching AnnaLise around the waist as she struggled. We ran up the stairs as Alice and others came out of their rooms.

Stella and I wrestled AnnaLise from Hadley and he collapsed against the rail, panting. AnnaLise was deadweight and we were glad when Logan lifted her in his arms and carried her back to the couple's room.

We helped Hadley back to the room and closed the door against prying eyes and ears. Their room happened to be a suite. Logan had taken AnnaLise and put her to bed. He asked Stella to sit with her.

Logan came back into the sitting room, and sternly addressed Hadley. "What was that all about?"

"Is she all right?" Hadley was shaking and had to sit down. "I thought she was going to jump over the railing."

"It looked to me like you were trying to push her down the stairs." I was being rough on the old man, but it looked like he was trying to kill his wife. His rich wife.

"NO. NO. I wouldn't do that. I love her. She is the light of my life. She was upset after the accident this afternoon and I gave her a sleeping pill to help her sleep. She was walking in her sleep. I swear it. If I hadn't woken up when she left the room . . ." He shuddered again and began to cry.

"I wouldn't hurt AnnaLise. I know her family think I married her for her money. But I didn't. We were childhood sweethearts. I've wanted nothing in this world but to love her and take care of her. Please believe me."

Suddenly I was aware of my pink granny gown and bare feet. I looked at Logan and he was looking at me. His white T-shirt and grey gym shorts showed he was very fit. At that moment, Stella came back into the room.

"She is asleep. I think she was sleepwalking. I don't think she will remember any of this in the morning.

Stella's tailored pajamas were a far cry from my granny gown. How did the woman sleep without mussing her hair? I scrubbed a hand through my unruly mop, that I'm sure was sticking up all over my head, and looked at my bare toes. I turned my toes up and wished I were anywhere but standing next to Mitch Logan.

Logan was laughing. "You are the height of fashion, granny," he said.

"Well, at least it is pink and has lace and it is warm." I mumbled.

He looked at Hadley. "Hadley, I want you to go back to bed and try to get some sleep." We'll see you in the morning."

"I won't sleep a wink." Hadley rubbed his face. "I'm afraid she will do it again."

"Lock the outside door and lock the bedroom door too. Put a chair beside her bed so she will make a noise if she gets up," Logan advised as Stella and I followed him out of the suite.

"Will she be safe with him?" I wasn't completely sure that Hadley was innocent.

"He's harmless. My office ran a more in depth check on him and AnnaLise. He signed a prenup when he married her. He will not inherit anything at her death. I think there is a monkey in the woodpile somewhere. You were sent to protect AnnaLise from Hadley, but it is possible someone else on this tour has an agenda for AnnaLise."

"I think we know who it is," I said, pulling him into our room. We think it is Billie Owensby. We filled him in our little trick.

"You could be right. I'll call my office as soon as I get back to my room and have her checked out more thoroughly."

He paused a moment with his hand on the door. Grinning he said, "Your gown reminds me of my boyhood days when I visited my granny."

I slammed the door – hard – behind him as he exited quickly.

Chapter 12

After our disturbing night, I didn't want to rise and shine. Stella, on the other hand, rose and was out the door early. She woke me coming in just before time to catch a ride for the jaunting car.

"I knew you wouldn't be up. You lazy writer." Get up. Get up. I brought coffee. You have thirty minutes before the jaunting car leaves. Drink your coffee, get in the shower."

"Go away."

"You can't miss this."

"What makes you so chipper?"

"The air. This wonderful Irish air."

I dragged my behind out of bed and headed for the shower, accepting the coffee she held out.

"I'll lay out your jeans and sweat shirt. It is cool out. You'll need your windbreaker too. We are scheduled for a boat ride. Don't wash your hair. You'll catch your death if your hair is wet."

"Can't hear you. The shower is running."

"Whatever."

After I dressed, I thanked her for the coffee and the roll she had brought from the breakfast bar. I grabbed a camera, my notebook and some tootsie rolls, and ran for the Jaunting car lineup.

"The jacket and sweatshirt feels just right." I commented to Stella, again thanking her for her earlier advice.

"An open air buggy ride and then a boat ride will be chilly." Stella pulled on a jacket over a sweatshirt too.

Do you have your camera, and notebook?" I asked unnecessarily knowing Stella would not go anywhere without her camera.

"Remember your Tootsie Rolls," she teased.

McKinnon prepared us well by giving his usual little speech before the Jaunting Car arrived. "The Jaunting Cars are a tradition here since Victorian times. For tourists, the Jaunting Cars are horse drawn open carriages, holding several people seated on either side." I was disappointed. I'd hoped for a Jaunting Car like Maureen O'Hara rode in the movie *The Quiet Man.* In our case, jarvies or drivers drove the Jaunting Car.

"Mr. and Mrs. King are keeping to their rooms this morning after her accident yesterday. She is okay, just needs a rest. Our tourist, Mr. Logan had business to attend to in Killarney."

I had not noticed Logan's absence. I looked around nervously, hoping my assailant and Stella's attacker at St. Kevin's was far away by now. Billiee Owensby was not with us either.

As the horses clomped around Killarney National Park, our jarvey kept up a running commentary about the park and what we were seeing.

"Sounds like he kissed the Blarney Stone, doesn't it? I don't know whether to look, take a picture or write in my notebook." I was frustrated.

"There is so much to see." someone agreed, as we looked here and there trying to catch everything.

As usual, Maureen complained. "No one told me it would be so cold. Vernon, why didn't you tell me to wear something warmer? This seat is hard. I need a cushion."

Stella rolled her eyes at me, then focused on three small Sitka deer near the tree line.

"I hope I'm getting all this down." I scratched away hurrying to get all the information written down. Rare Kerry Blue cattle. The Macgillycuddy Mountains. Too much information. "The next problem will be reading it afterwards."

I stopped writing when a rugged castle beside the lake came into view. The jarvey informed us it is the Ross Castle built in the 15th century by the O'Donoghues. It was the last stronghold in Ireland to be taken by Cromwell's Army. Knowing the castle couldn't be taken by land, the army stormed the castle from the seaside. The guards gave up without a fight.

"Oh, my, Stella, get some shots of that. It is beautiful with the lake beside it." I knew I did not need to instruct Stella where to focus her camera. I also I knew I couldn't do the scene justice with my small digital.

Stella obediently shot the castle and lake from several angles.

"I think the group is headed for the boat now, Stella." I didn't want to be left too far behind the others since Logan wasn't around to protect us.

"I keep thinking someone is watching us, waiting to pounce." I communicated my fears to Stella.

"I know. I feel the same way. I keep looking around, not really knowing what I'm looking for."

The writer's mode kicked into gear again when I saw the name of boat, *Lilly of Killarney*. "That would be a good name for a character in a book."

"It will also be a title for the picture I took of the boat with the lake and the mountains in the background." Stella kept clicking away.

The boat captain began to talk about the fish in the lake and the other two lakes known as the Lakes of Killarney. I listened but didn't take notes. I was lost in dreams until he pointed out the ruins of Innisfallen Abbey. Now this was something I could use.

I took careful notes. "That is Innisfallin Island. St. Fenian the Leper also built the first abbey in the 7th century. The ruins of Innisfallin Abbey you see there are from the 11th and 12th century. For 1000 years, it was known as the seat of learning. We are floating on Lough Leanne. The lake got its name from the Abbey. Lough Leanne means Lake of Learning. Monks recording the early history of Ireland wrote the Annals of Innisfallen."

The boat ride was interesting. The guide was first a guide, then a fisherman and answered many questions from the men in the tour. Animals on the shore were visible as were many dwellings. However, there is something about being on the water that makes one hungry.

The Jaunting Car delivered us at the pub where we had reservations for lunch. Traditional Irish stew was on the menu. Potatoes, carrots and onions stewed with mutton were delicious and warming.

"May I have your attention, please?" McKinnon didn't usually join us for meals. He preferred the bar. "I want to introduce our hosts here at Muckross Park Hotel, Bill Cullen and Jackie Lavin."

After polite applause, Cullen welcomed us. "Muckross Park Hotel dates back to 1795. We are located on 25,000 acres National Park. You saw some of the park this morning on the Jaunting Car tour and aboard the *Lilly of Killarney.* Queen Victoria took tea here in 1861, George Bernard Shaw wrote *Pygmalion* here in the summer of 1925. It later became *My Fair Lady* of which I'm sure you are familiar. I inherited Muckross Park Hotel from my grandmother Moll Darcy. My partner and I have kept the Victorian décor combining it with modern facilities. I hope you enjoy your stay here. Be sure to visit our gift shop. You will find the story of my life there; *It's a Long Way from Penny Apples.* In it, you will appreciate the long struggle out of poverty to what you see today.

More applause and we settled down for a dessert custard. Afterwards, some of the group took the opportunity to go into Killarney for shopping.

"I'm still a bit chilly," I told Stella. "I think I'd

like to go to the room and nap awhile."

"That sounds like a good plan," she said. "I want to check out the gift shop. I want to buy Mr. Cullen's book and more postcards."

"You have mailed postcards to everyone you know." I enjoyed teasing Stella.

She was learning to come back at me. "Have not. I know a lot of people."

The gift shop was a delight. While Stella purchased her cards and the book, I wandered around shopping. Seeing Rose and Curtis across the room, I started to speak to them, when I saw Rose pick up an inexpensive stuffed leprechaun and put it in her pocket.

Surprised, I glanced at Curtis. He caught my eye and bowed his head. He took the toy from her pocket, gently saying, "We must pay for this, dear." Rose acted like nothing unusual had happened.

Stella, I, and a few from our group strolled toward our annex, intent on getting some rest. Several Guardia cars and an Emergency Response Unit blocked our way.

"What is going on?" Maureen's words were loud and clear. Others murmured among themselves. I saw fear in Stella's eyes and I'm sure it was mirrored in mine.

A female Guarda stopped us before we reached the blockade. "Can you tell us what is going on?" I hoped I managed to keep the fear from my voice.

"No, Ma'am. I cannot. Please go back into the hotel proper until we come for you."

"Is American Agent Mitch Logan in there?"

"Yes, he is. He is assisting our agency in an

investigation."

"Is he alright?" Fear thinned my voice to a squeak. "The emergency vehicle is not for him?"

"It is not for him."

"Is he available? May I speak with him one moment?"

She motioned to another uniformed officer toward the annex. I gasped in relief to see Logan coming toward us.

He spoke to the group gawking, stretching their necks to see what was happening behind the vehicles.

"Please go back into the hotel. Everyone stay there until someone comes for you." To me he said, "I need you to do something for me."

"What is happening? What can I do?"

"I need you to make a list of everyone that was on the tour with you this morning. Can you do that?"

"Of course I can do that. But please, please tell me what is happening?"

He put a hand on my shoulder. "It is bad. AnnaLise and Hadley were murdered this morning."

Shocked, I put my hand over my mouth to keep from screaming as tears sprang to my eyes.

"Please do not tell anyone right now. I will be with you in a short while to answer your questions, Now get this group out of here and into a room in the hotel."

"I must tell Stella," I whispered.

"Okay, but no one else. Understand?"

I nodded, unable to comprehend what had

happened to the old couple.

Stella took my arm as we started back to the hotel proper. She knew, instinctively, that something terrible was wrong. "Can you tell me what he said?"

"Yes, but not until we are alone." By this time, tears were running down my cheeks. "Let's sit out in the little arbor garden awhile."

The arbor garden was small, private and beautiful. The scent of many flowers made it a popular place to relax. Fortunately, no one was there when Stella and I entered it. Tinkling water from a fountain was soothing. I sat down and drew Stella down with me.

Drawing her close to me, I struggled with the words. *Inhale, exhale, inhale, breathe.* "Logan said Hadley and AnnaLise were murdered this morning."

"Murdered?" She was shocked as I was. We sat for a long minute sharing the heat of each other's arms and grieving for the old couple.

"Did Logan say how?"

"No, He said he would come to the hotel soon and tell everyone. In the meantime, he asked that we not tell anyone. I guess all of us are suspects, because he asked me to make a list of all the people with us this morning."

"That would be nearly everyone in the tour."

"I noticed Logan wasn't there nor was Billie Owensby. I'll have to think if anyone else didn't go. I remember Maureen complaining."

"Let's go inside, Lacey. You are cold. We can write a list inside." She helped me to rise.

"I don't know if I'm shaking from cold or from shock."

"Maybe we can rustle up some hot tea or something." I was thankful for Stella's caring attitude.

Inside the building, I pulled her into a restroom, opened the booth, sat on a stool and cried. Stella was patient and waited for me. After I cried myself out, one look in the mirror told me I looked horrible. I washed my face with cold water, dabbing at my swelling red eyes. Some people can cry and still look beautiful. Not me, I blubber, my nose ran and my eyes swelled.

"I don't have any makeup in my bag, do you?" I asked Stella.

"I never carry makeup on these outings. It makes my carry bag or purse too heavy."

"Well, I'll just have to face the mob, looking like this."

Our group was in a lobby, away from the general public. They stood around, gossiping, acting bored. They didn't pay any attention to Stella or me. We sat down apart from everyone.

I got my notebook and pen out of my carry bag. I tried to begin a list. Finally, I asked Stella, "Would you do this, please. My hand is shaking so I can't write legibly." Writing about murder is a lot easier than experiencing it.

She took the notebook and together we discussed who was with us on the morning trip. Everyone was accounted for except Logan and Billie Owensby.

I looked at Stella with a question in my eyes.

"Could she...?"

"Don't borrow trouble. Wait for Logan." At this point, Stella was the calm one.

After awhile, the group became restless. Maureen was her usual self demanding answers of no one and receiving answers of no one. The Pages were placating although they knew nothing either.

I sat with head down, shading my swollen, red eyes and thought about AnnaLise. I was supposed to protect her. I failed. Because I didn't do my job, she died. Presently, someone brought in tea, coffee and pastries.

"You look like you could use something hot to drink ." Alice was holding out two cups. "What's wrong, dear? Are you coming down with a cold from the cold air this morning?

"Uh, yes. A cold or allergy or something." I'm not a good liar.

"Well, this should help or would you rather have tea? I wish they would hurry over there so we can get back into our rooms. I need some medicine. I didn't take it with me because I planned to be back in my room in time to take it."

"This is fine, Alice. I'm sure they won't be long now." Stella saved me from talking any more.

The hot coffee revived me and I quit sniffling. I could tell others were becoming bored and I could understand why. We had been in this room more than two hours.

Logan came into the room. McKinnon and a couple of uniformed Guardia accompanied him. I wanted to know what he had to say, but I dreaded to hear it.

I pulled Alice down beside me and held her hand. I didn't want her to be alone when she heard about AnnaLise and Hadley.

McKinnon spoke first. "Folks, I have some bad news. You noticed the Guardia here and the Emergency Response Unit. I'm sorry to tell you that our friends, Hadley and AnnaLise King were murdered this morning."

A collective gasp and clamor rose up all over the room. "What happened?" "Are we in danger?" "Who did it?" "How did it happen?"

I wanted to know all those things too, but common sense told me we would not get answers from the cops before the cops got answers from us.

"Calm down." Logan made quieting motions with his hands. "I am special agent Mitch Logan from USA Homeland security working with a counter-terrorism detail here in Ireland."

Again, an unrestrained clamor all over the room. "Are we in danger?" "Terrorism." "No." "Hadley and AnnaLise?" "I can't believe it."

Maureen was loudest of all. "I demand you send us home immediately. This is ridiculous."

"Calm down." Logan's voice was loud over the din. I can't answer your questions now. The police here will question each of you. Do not be afraid. This is routine. We need to know what you know or what you may have seen. We will question each of you separately. Mr. McKinnon has a word for you, then I will call each of you into another room for a statement. Lacey James and Stella Gerritson, I will talk with you first." I felt two dozen eyes boring into my back. Did they think we had something to do with the murders?

McKinnon raised his voice. "The hotel regrets the inconvenience at this time. You may go back into your rooms to pack, then you will be assigned a different room. This is an upsetting situation. Try to relax while the police work it all out. As soon as you are through with your statements to the Guarda, you will be accompanied to your rooms to pack. After that you are free until dinner, which will be in the same dining room as last night. Again, I cannot tell you how much I regret the circumstances. In all the time I have been escorting tours, this has never happened to me."

The room was quiet as Stella and I followed Logan and one of the Guarda into the next room.

"Have you got that list for me?" Logan asked. To the policeman he said, "This is the ladies I told you about, Lacey James and Stella Gerritson. They were on the tour this morning and have made a list of those also on the tour."

"Everyone was on the tour except you and Billie Owensby." Stella handed the list to him.

"Billie didn't do this," he said abruptly. "She is in custody for the attempted murder of AnnaLise by pushing her into the road yesterday."

I'm sure my mouth fell open. "How. . .?"

"I contacted my people who discovered you were right. She did not come from Sedona, Arizona. She has a rap sheet a mile long. When we confronted her, she confessed that Hadley's cousins hired her to kill AnnaLise. They planned for Hadley to inherit millions, then they would take care of Hadley.

"I must ask for your discretion about what I have told you. Also, please do not tell anyone, I say anyone, about the possibility of extremists in the area. All they need to know is I am an American who happened to be here when the Kings were killed. Got that?"

"Of course." We both agreed. But I ventured further, "I must call AnnaLise's sister and niece. They have to be told."

"An agent has notified them. You may use my cell phone to call them when we are finished here."

"How did you know who to call?"

"AnnaLise's next of kin was written on her tour information."

"I have more bad news. I can't shield you from this. We think the person who wants the microchip killed AnnaLise and Hadley. Your room was trashed. Not just trashed, destroyed. There is nothing left of your personal belongings. We believe Hadley and AnnaLise saw the person or persons entering your room. It looks like AnnaLise was thrown down the stairs. Her neck was broken. Hadley apparently ran from the assailant and was stabbed in the back. They both died instantly. I'm sorry to have to lay this on you right now. You two are in danger. Whoever this is wants that microchip enough to murder for it. If they didn't find it in your room, they will be after you, Lacey, and maybe Stella if they can't get to you. I want you to stay together. Either a plainclothes police officer or I will be near you all the time. You must be quiet about all this."

I began to weep. I couldn't help it. He laid his

hand on my shoulder. "Keep a stiff upper lip. We'll find this guy, I promise." The warmth of his touch was consoling.

Chapter 13

Calling A.P. was the hardest thing I've ever done. I blubbered and sniffled and she did too. "I'm so sorry A.P. AnnaLise was a sweet lady. She didn't deserve to die. I didn't protect her. I'm so sorry." And I cried some more.

"You couldn't know what would happen and you couldn't be with them every minute. I didn't expect you to." She became calmer. "What exactly is going on there, Lacey?"

"I can't tell you now, A.P. I'll tell you as soon as everything is explained. Stella and I will accompany the bodies home. I owe them that." I shuddered again but didn't cry.

"I appreciate that, Lacey. That might console my mother."

"How is your mother?"

"Physically she is progressing. She is in rehab. She is broken about AnnaLise's death. They were close. I must go, Lacey. Please don't blame yourself for all this."

I hung up the phone and burst into tears again. Stella was a rock, staying with me, handing me tissues. "I feel so guilty," I sobbed.

"Lacey be real. You couldn't stay with them all the time. They wanted to rest this morning. It was natural that we go ahead with the tour."

I looked at her with bleary eyes and nodded. "Let's see if Logan will let us see the room. Maybe there is something we can salvage."

"Logan says everything was ruined." She gathered up the soggy tissues and looked for a waste receptacle.

Logan was right outside the door. He came to me immediately. "Are you okay?"

"No, but I will be. I'd like to see the room. See if anything can be salvaged."

"I'd rather you didn't, Lacey. Management has given you a suite in this building. An Irish agent or I will be with you at all times. I must remind you again, the two of you must stay together."

"The things those monsters destroyed belong to Stella and me. We deserve to see what they did."

He relented and motioned us to follow him. The Guardia were still working, the cars were still blocking the road to the annex. He led us into the door. The stairs went to the second floor from here and the first floor hall led to the left and right. Our room was straight ahead.

I averted my eyes from the stairs but my thoughts were on frail AnnaLise and the terror she must have felt as she fell. I was aware of the odor of blood and death and shuddered. Logan opened the door to our room.

Shock is not the word for it. I have never seen such destruction. The bed was stripped, Our mattresses in tatters, chairs were overturned, and the undersides ripped open. Our suitcases were cut to pieces. Clothes were everywhere. They were cut or torn. Not a whole piece of clothing remained.

I leaned against the wall, surveying the damage. Everything was gone. Stella stepped carefully between the piles of clothing, looking for something. I don't know what.

There was nothing valuable in my possessions. But they were mine and someone destroyed them. That made me angry. Shreds of the galley copies of my book were scattered over everything. Seeing the destruction made me mad.

"The terrorists want that microchip and will do anything to get it. I wish you were not involved in this." Logan seemed genuinely sorry.

I turned toward the bathroom. It had not escaped. Lotion and shampoo bottles had been cut open, their contents dumped. Makeup, pills, and deodorant received the same treatment.

I picked a hairbrush from behind the commode. I could use it again if I washed it. But did I want to?

"Leave it all, Lacey. The hotel has insurance to replace damaged luggage. My agency will advance you some money if you need it."

I struggled to comprehend what he was saying. "Yes," I said vaguely. "We need to shop." I turned to Stella. "There isn't anything left."

I saw tears in her eyes. "We have our life,

Lacey. We have the things in our carry bags and purses. We can do this, Lacey."

"Unless the murderers found what they were looking for, they will be back. The complete destruction leads me to believe they didn't find the microchip. If they had found it, they would have stopped looking. But they continued to tear into everything.

An officer will drive you into Killarney. Do you need to go to your room first?" Logan said.

"Yes." Stella was firm. Let us settle a bit. We'll be ready in an hour."

A female officer escorted us to our assigned room. It was more luxurious than the one we had in the annex. "My name is Arlene. I'll just wait here in the living area while you rest, then I will drive you to Killarney. I'll be on duty until midnight." She was a pleasant lass about twenty-five. She looked strong but not tough.

Stella and I retreated to the bedroom area. Twin beds were inviting, but we sank into matching chairs and looked at each other.

"Stella, I am so sorry I got you into this."

"You didn't know all this would happen. If we get out of this alive, we'll have a great story to tell our grandkids."

"My grandkids will not believe this story. They will think it is my writer's imagination working overtime."

"We can't do much to freshen up, except wash." Stella looked at me. "And your face could sure use a wash." She smiled as she said it.

"Right, and you think your face looks any

better. You need to do something before Rory sees you again, or he will run clear back to Dublin."

And that is the way we got through the evening. We put on a cheerful face and joked.

Chapter 14

"The last thing I want to do is to shop. I'd like to just crawl into bed, pull the covers over my head and cry. I keep seeing poor AnnaLise going over that banister and the blood after Hadley was stabbed. I never want to write about murder again."

Stella looked as tired as I felt. "Hiding in the room won't help. We need some necessities. Let's take an inventory and see what we have." She followed words with action, dumping out her purse and carry bag on her bed.

"I'll need a list. I'm so tired, I'll forget half what I need without a list." I dumped my purse and carry bag out beside Stella's.

"Not much there." I separated out my notebook, camera, scarf, tootsie rolls and three pens.

"Stella, is this your pen?" I held up a chunky,

tri-shaped pen.

"No, I brought cheapies with me. I lose them all the time." Stella glanced at the pen and went on sorting her belongings.

"Well, it isn't mine. I never buy chunky pens either. I would never buy one shaped like that. I like slim line pens. How did it get in my bag?"

Stella looked at me. "Do you think. . .?"

"I think we need to call Logan."

I peeked into the living area. "Arlene, could you call Logan for us? We need to see him immediately."

"Of course." She reached for her radio. We were startled at a soft knock on the door. She motioned Stella and me back into the bedroom. Peeking out, we saw her open the door quickly. Stella had a grip on my hand that was sure to leave bruises. Three of us breathed a sigh of relief to see the valet. He offered Arlene a basket with the explanation, "Management would like to present this to Ms. James and Ms. Gerritson with our compliments."

"Thank you, I'll see they get it." Arlene took the proffered basket and closed the door. She sat it gingerly on a nearby table, grabbed her radio and summoned Logan. "Need you immediately. A basket has been delivered. It should be examined."

We heard Logan's response, "Be right there. Don't touch anything."

Stella and I still cowered behind the door and Arlene backed toward our hiding place. "Get as far away as you can. Go into the bathroom and close the door." She ordered.

We obeyed.

Stella sat on the commode and I sat on the edge of the bathtub, holding my head in my hands. "What else can happen to us?"

Stella patted my shoulder. "Where is the pen?"

"In my pocket."

About five minutes later, Logan knocked softly and opened the door. "You can come out now. Bill sent the gift, thinking of things you may need. It's clean."

To Arlene he said, "You were on top of it. That is good."

Stella was examining the gift basket. "Bill Cullen or his wife is thoughtful. Anyway, look at this Lacey. They sent shampoo, conditioner, lotion, soap, tooth brushes and toothpaste, even some chocolates." She opened the package and passed around dark chocolate truffles.

I remembered the pen at the same time I took a bite. "Logan," I mumbled.

"Yes," he mumbled back mocking my chocolate mouthful.

Arlene giggled, Stella joined her and soon all of us were laughing.

Swallowing the delicious bite of candy, I said, "We found something." I pulled the pen from my pocket. "It isn't mine or Stella's. Could it be what they were looking for?"

He took it carefully in his hand and examined it. "It could be. Why didn't we find this before?" *Was he suspicious of me?*

"I don't know. Look, I haven't been holding out on you. Maybe it was stuck in the lining of the bag. Maybe we overlooked it when we searched before."

"Which bag was it in?" His question was curt.

"I really don't know. I dumped my carry bag and my purse out on the bed at the same time, and there it was."

"This may be the source of all our problems." He studied it intently. "I'll get it down to Dublin and have it analyzed.

"Thanks, Lacey. I'm so relieved. I think you've found the microchip." His eyes crinkled as his mouth relaxed into a grin.

"You mean it? Hooray! Now go tell those mean old terrorists, I don't have their microchip and tell them to please leave us alone now." I was babbling from relief. It was over. No more looking over my shoulder at every stranger.

"It's not quite that simple, but it's a start. Are you ready to go shopping?"

"We didn't have time to make a list, but let's get this done." I was resigned. "I hate shopping."

"Most women like shopping." He was teasing me again.

"I'm not most women." I was too grumpy to be teased.

"Have another chocolate truffle, grab your jacket, and let's go." Arlene held the door. I scrambled to put my wallet and tootsie rolls back in my purse.

Logan locked the door and gave Stella the key. On the way to the car, Craig Cranfield barred my way.

"What do you want?" I snarled.

"Lacey, I need to talk to you for a minute." The others had gone on ahead. I didn't want to be alone with this man.

"Look, lover boy. What you do in the dark with your best friend's wife is none of my business." Now leave me alone."

"Please don't tell Linda." He was actually whining.

"I do not intend to tell your wife or anyone what I saw on the stairs that night. I suggest you stop the nonsense. It is immature and belittling. Your wife doesn't deserve you. Now get out of my way, I have things that are more important on my mind than a two-timer like you. I barreled ahead.

CHAPTER 15

People stared as we hurried toward the police car in the drive. Did they think we were being arrested? I felt guilty. Not guilty like a fugitive. Guilty like I had failed AnnaLise. I would always carry the burden of failure of protecting that frail little lady. I couldn't look anyone in the eye.

Irene Bouchard was standing next to the police car. She wore jeans, a dark colored hooded jacket and tennis shoes. She pleaded with Arlene. "Please let me go with you. I'm so bored and shopping with you girls would be so much fun."

Girls, I hadn't been a girl in a long time.

Arlene began making excuses. "This is a rush trip. We won't have time for dinner. Stella and Lacey just need a few things. I'm sure you'll be more comfortable staying here at the hotel."

I saw Logan give Arlene a nod. I glared at him. If he thought I would enjoy having this tourist guide trainee help me shop, he was wrong.

Arlene relented. "Okay, get in. Let's go. I'd like to get home sometime tonight."

Irene preempted the front seat, so Stella and I slid into the back seat. Arlene drove well, but fast. I guess she really did want to finish this little shopping trip so she could get home.

She pulled into a mall area. "This is the outlet center. You should be able to get anything you want here. If not, we'll try somewhere else." She looked at Stella and me. "Please stay together."

"Of course, we'll stay together," Irene said. "I know exactly what these girls need and I know value when I see it. We really don't need you, Officer. Why don't you get a cup of coffee or something? We'll be fine."

Arlene followed us into the first store. I felt nervous, knowing someone had destroyed our things and might still be after us. The first purchases were easy. I'm not a good shopper when I'm not in the mood and I definitely was not in the mood. I grabbed makeup, underwear, socks, and pajamas as quickly as I could throw them in the cart. I smiled, remembering Logan's comment about my granny gown, as I chose a pair of tailored pajamas in a vibrant purple. I'll bet his granny never wore purple pajamas.

Stella and I stayed close together and Irene stayed on our heels.

"I like these slacks." Stella held up a pair of dark green pants.

"We need slacks, a dressy jacket and another shirt to go with jeans." I was trying hard to concentrate. "Another pair of shoes, and we must get a new suitcases."

A black and grey tweed pantsuit was my size. I added a beige blouse to go with it.

"Not that blouse." Irene pulled it from my basket and substituted an orange turtleneck sweater.

"That is not really my style." I replaced the sweater on the rack and began searching for another blouse or sweater. Stella was adding clothes to the basket. A short jacket with green and brown would go with the slacks she picked out earlier. A flared brown skirt would pair with the jacket also.

"I really don't see anything I like." I wasn't in the shopping mood and therefore nothing looked good to me. I jerked a white man-tailored blouse off the rack and threw it in the basket. A maroon sweater with a cowl neck followed a black turtleneck sweater into the basket.

"Try this on," Irene held up a floral skirt. "It would look good with a jean jacket or a sweater."

"Oh, I don't think so." I barely looked at the skirt.

"I insist." Something in her voice made me look at her. She held the skirt folded over her arm hiding her hand. I could see the small bore of the pistol she held, pointed straight at me. I looked for Arlene. She and Stella were several yards away, looking at a rack of jackets. Neither were looking toward Irene and me."

"You?" I stammered in surprise.

"Yes, me. Now move slowly toward the dressing rooms at the back of the store."

I looked back at my friend and the guarda, still

engrossed in conversation.

"Move!" Her voice was low but insistent.

I moved. Head down, trying to think how to get myself out of this predicament.

"Now walk past the dressing rooms to the back door. Easy now and no one will get hurt." Irene was close behind. She the pushed back door open to reveal a sleek black sedan waiting there, it's door standing open. She roughly shoved me inside. "Move O'Shea," was the last words I heard. I felt a pin prick in my thigh and blacked out.

Chapter 16

I didn't want to wake up. It was cozy here in this dark place. Someone was prodding my shoulder. I turned and pulled my knees and hugged them. Yucky smell, whew!

"Wake up and face the music. Wake up. Hey wake up."

"Where's the music?" My eyes wouldn't open.

"You gave her too much." It was a man's voice. The prodding started again. I opened my eyes to see Irene leaning over me, her face hateful and menacing.

"Ummm. Don't want to wake up."

"You better wake up before Kohane gets here or you'll wish you were awake and talking. He won't take any nonsense."

"Kohane? Ummm. Who is Kohane?"

"You don't need to know. Where is the microchip?"

"Let me sleep."

"Wake up, you thief and tell me where you hid the microchip."

"Don't have a microchip." I tried to go back to sleep.

"This will wake you up." She dashed cold water in my face. I sat up sputtering.

"Where am I?" I wiped the water from my eyes and looked around. I was sitting on a filthy mattress. Had I been lying on that piece of junk? I patted my clothes. I was still dressed although my jacket was wet.

"Where am I?" I repeated as I tried to get to my feet.

Irene shoved me back down on my behind and stood over me with the gun. "Where. Is. The. Microchip?"

"I don't have it."

"But you did have it?"

I was beginning to feel more coherent. "You didn't find it did you?" I turned to Irene. "You are despicable. You killed AnnaLise and Hadley. They didn't hurt you. You killed them because they were there."

"I didn't kill anybody. Remember I was with you on the tour." She laughed, taunting me.

A man came to the mattress. He was slightly built, with a beard and cold eyes. "Look, Missy. You better give us the microchip. Kohane don't let anybody live who messes with him."

"My name is Lacey and I don't know anyone named Kohane."

"You don't want to know him, Missy." He

sneered as he bit off the words and lit a cigarette.

"Please don't smoke in here." It was automatic. Something I said to anyone who lit up in front of me.

"Please don't smoke in here," he mocked me as he blew smoke in my face.

"I need a drink of water." My mouth felt like it was full of cotton or worse.

"Get it yourself." Irene gestured grandly to a dirty sink in the corner. It wasn't easy for me to get up from the floor but I managed, standing erect, dizziness hit me and I nearly fell. Neither Irene nor her partner offered to help me. A rickety chair was between the sink and me. If I can get to that chair, *I can hang on to it.* I took a few staggering steps, my head was spinning but I grabbed the back of the chair. It was so wiggly, I thought it wouldn't hold my weight, but it did. From there, I went to the sink and turned on the water.

"Let's go get some coffee," Irene said to the man. "Maybe when she wakes up a little more, she'll be more cooperative. Kohane should be here with Logan within the hour, so we have time to question her before he gets here."

Logan coming here. Was he with the killers? No. He couldn't be. He already has the microchip. He wouldn't be coming here to get it from me. They were planning to kidnapping Logan too. This Kohane would kill us both.

They left the room and I heard the lock turn in the door. The sink had years of grime on it. A thin stream of cold water was enough to wash my hands. I drank from them in huge gulps, then scrubbed my face and dried it on my shirt tail. I held on to the sink and looked around at my prison.

The room, most likely in an old house, I concluded, was filthy. A single, bare light bulb hung from the ceiling. A dirty string served as a pull chain. At least they didn't turn off the light. The dirty mattress and the rickety chair was the only furniture in the room. Only one window and it was boarded over.

I made my unsteady way to the window and pulled at the boards. Someone had used heavy boards and plenty of nails. No way was I going to be able to pull those boards off. Is that traffic I heard? Maybe we are still in Killarney. They could have taken me anywhere. I had no idea how long I'd been out. One hour until Kohane comes to threaten me. Was Kohane the head of the terrorist cell in Dublin? But Irene and skinny guy would come back before that.

"Think Lacey. Do something." I muttered.

I slowly walked to the door and tried the knob. Locked as I knew it would be. I could hear Irene and skinny guy talking. Think! Think! I need to do something when they enter the room and run out. "Ha. Fat chance." My voice sounded hoarse.

I went back to the sink, feeling more steady on my feet. *I* needed a weapon. I searched my pockets. Nothing there but Tootsie Rolls and tissues. Not even a pen. I laughed out loud at the irony. A pen caused all this and I didn't even have a pen for a measly weapon. Probably wouldn't work anyway. Think! What would a heroine in your book do to get out of this locked room? I stuffed a couple of tootsie rolls in my mouth for courage.

Could I dismantle the sink drain? I got down on my knees. The fittings were rusty but refused to budge. I tried the window again. Pulling and tugging at the boards to no avail. Whoever nailed the boards across the window didn't intend for them to be pulled off.

My gaze wandered to the chair – the rickety chair. It was about to fall down. What if I helped it fall apart? I quietly turned it on the side, testing the legs one by one. I found the one that wiggled the most and tugged on it. The leg came away from the seat with a screech, a wicked looking nail stuck into the end. A couple of small nails came loose as well.

I listened for a few seconds, expecting Irene and her friend to come in to investigate the noise. They continued to talk and laugh in the next room. I worked the little nails loose and held them in my hand. They weren't much of a weapon but maybe if I aimed for the eyes. But this chair leg. I could use it like a baseball bat on the first person in the room, then run past the person and hopefully out the door. Probably get shot in the process. Better to die in action than waiting for the inevitable.

I stationed myself by the door, hefting the chair leg in two hands and waited.

It seemed like I stood there a lifetime, tense and shaking. Sweat poured off me. Can I do this? Can I hit another human hard enough to do harm? You betcha! If it meant a chance to escape.

I heard scuffling noises on the other side of the door. They were coming for me. I planted my feet and drew back the chair leg bat. The door opened and I closed my eyes and struck out as hard as I could.

"Oof!" But the person didn't fall, he only bent double, turned and grabbed me around the waist. I struggled, hitting out with hands and feet.

"Lacey! Stop fighting. It's me, Logan."

I looked up into Logan's eyes. "Jeez, Louise! Did you have to hit me?" He wrestled the chair leg from me. "A nail. You could've killed me."

"I meant to hurt somebody. I didn't know it was you. I thought it was Skinny Guy or Irene. How did you know where they brought me?"

"I followed them. I was in the alley when Irene pushed you out that door and into the back of the car. It was easy to follow them here. This old house is not far from the city center."

"You used me as bait? How could you? You let them drug me and keep me here. What took you so long?" I was so angry I was incoherent.

"Calm down. I didn't use you as bait?"

"Calm down. They could have killed me in this place. You only wanted to catch the terrorist. You didn't care that they brought me here. They were planning to kill me." Angry tears streamed down my face.

"Lacey. Lacey. I knew where they brought you. They wanted the microchip. They wouldn't take a chance of killing you if you knew where it was. I called for backup and we came in as soon as Kohane showed up. We got them all."

"I can't believe you put my life in danger to catch them." I couldn't stop the angry tears. I needed to sit down, but there was nothing in the room but a broken chair and a filthy mattress. I pushed past Logan into the other room to find it full of people. Three of them were handcuffed, the others had badges. This room was as dismal as the one where I was held. It had a swaybacked couch with the stuffing falling out, a couple of wooden boxes and an old refrigerator.

Logan placed his hand on my elbow, but I refused his help and stormed out of the front door. I looked around at the neighborhood. The dilapidated house looked like its neighbors but the moon in the clear sky was a welcome sight. I took great gulping breaths of night air. "Can I go now?"

"I'll take you back to the hotel. Stella is waiting for you there."

"Is Stella okay?"

"Yes, she is frantic about you and Arlene will never forgive herself for letting you out of her sight. My man phoned them as soon as we knew you were safe."

"I may never speak to you again, for leaving me in this place." I hiccupped.

When I reached the hotel, I fell into Stella's arms, both of us crying. "I'm okay," I assured her.

"I'll take care of her now," Stella said to Logan and Arlene.

"I'll bring something from the pub. She hasn't eaten and you hardly ate any dinner either." Arlene patted my back sympathetically.

Stella led me to the bathroom and turned on the hot water. "That looks so good. I feel nasty dirty. Stella, there was this awful, filthy mattress..."

"Shh. I can imagine. You smell like a brewery

and a pub full of cigarette smokers. Relax. I'll get your clothes."

"My clothes. I didn't buy any clothes. She, Irene, took me." I couldn't finish the sentence. The shock of the kidnapping was more than I could explain. Tears bubbled up again.

I bought the things you had picked out and added a few things. You have what you need. Now get into the bath."

I sank into the hot water with fragrant bubbles up to my neck. I smelled so bad, I could smell myself. I reached for the shampoo. It felt so good to be clean. A huge heated white towel waited.

Stella stuck her head in with the purple p.j.'s.

Arlene arrived with broccoli-cheddar soup, crusty fresh bread and tea accompanied with a decadent chocolate layer cake for desert, as I vigorously towel dried my hair.

"Ah, it is good to feel clean again."

"Ah, it is good not having to smell you anymore," Stella joked. "I'll throw these nasty clothes in the trash."

Arlene lingered beside the door as I began my delayed supper. "I'll tell you good night. I may not see you again before you go home. I wish you luck. I am so sorry I failed to protect you."

"Will you be disciplined?" I asked.

"If I am I deserve it, but I think they will be so happy to crack this case, they will ignore my lowly state." She smiled. "May I say, I like the purple jammies.

CHAPTER 17

Stella and I debated whether to show up for breakfast with the tour. We had a restless night. My body was sore and bruised. I'm sure I disturbed Stella as I tossed and turned, picturing the gory details of Hadley and AnnaLise's untimely murders.

A hot shower and a bit of makeup to cover the bags under my eyes made me presentable. I hoped a cup of strong Irish coffee would keep my eyes open and my mouth shut.

The new clothes felt stiff and uncomfortable, but there was no help for that. We both chose khakis and sweaters with soft boots.

A murmur rose from the tour group when we appeared in the dining room but Alice quickly made room for us at her table and offered to get coffee for us. We gratefully accepted.

Various members of the group stopped by the table to offer their comments saying how sorry they were that I was abducted. Maureen as usual was caustic, "Bad things happen when you are in wrong places."

Jo Fletcher was kinder, "Really Maureen. She was in a shopping mall."

Maureen lifted her head with a sneer, "Well, these days you never know."

McKinnon interrupted our breakfast with an announcement. "Experience European Tours regret the tragic circumstances that took our friends, AnnaLise and Hadley. We have decided it best that we end the tour here in Killarney. Please accept our voucher for another tour with Experience European in the future. Take the morning to explore Killarney. I have arranged a pub lunch for you in Killarney. The bus will leave at 10:00 for a short sight-seeing tour before lunch. Be ready to meet the bus at 3 p.m. to Shannon airport. See me after breakfast for vouchers and plane tickets.

"Well, how about that? Two trips for the price of one." Maureen smiled showing a full set of dentures.

"How can she be so happy after all that has happened?" I asked to anyone who was listening.

"Just consider the source and don't worry about it," Stella soothed.

"I'm happy to leave. This trip has been jinxed from the start," was April's comment.

Alice Baker poured more tea and said, "I'll be back. Ireland is a fascinating place and we haven't seen nearly all of it."

"Stella, I think I will stay here at the hotel. I'm weary. Even my bones are tired. I'll take a cab into

Killarney for lunch. We need new suitcases. I'll get them and anything else we need. I need to call A.P. and firm up the arrangements to fly AnnaLise and Hadley's bodies home.

"Rest as much as you can. My things are ready to go except for putting them in the suitcase."

I instructed Stella to take pictures on the sightseeing trip and waved as the bus pulled out.

As I turned back toward the hotel, I saw Curtis Edington sitting on a bench nearby. He looked like he had lost his last friend. I walked over to him and sat down. "Curtis, is something wrong?"

When he raised his head, I saw tears on his cheeks.

I took his old, wrinkled hand. "What is wrong? Let me help."

"I don't know what to do. I don't know who can help. I guess I have to tell someone."

"Tell someone? Is Rose okay? Where is she?"

"She's in the room. She thought she needed to do her nails."

"Well, then, what can be so bad?"

He stumbled over the words as he spoke. "Rose has a problem. I've covered for her all our married life. Tried to pay for what she took, tried to smooth it over with people."

"I suspected as much. You are a good man. The word for Rose's problem is kleptomania. That is a disease. She can't help what she does."

"I've returned everything she took while on the trip or paid for it. But I don't know what to do about the ring."

"She took a ring?" Then the light dawned on

me. "She took Maureen's ring?"

"Yes, I have it. She didn't even know when I took it from her purse. But, if I return it to Maureen, she will make a fuss. She might even call the police. I couldn't stand that and Rose wouldn't understand.

"Help me, Lacey. Tell me what to do. I must do something today."

We sat there for a few minutes commiserating together. Then I said, "Give the ring to me. I will get it back to Maureen and she won't have a clue that Rose took it."

"But they will blame you."

"Stella and I will figure out something."

He breathed a sigh of relief, took the ring from his pocket and dropped it in my hand.

It was a beautiful ring and very expensive. No doubt, Maureen would call the Guarda if she suspected Rose stole the ring. How could I protect her and myself?

Curtis rose from the bench and I watched him walk toward the hotel as if the weight of the world was on his shoulders. I could relate. I felt the same weight on my shoulders. I had to call A.P. and call the police station before I went into Killarney.

Why did I take on the burden of the ring too? How am I going to return it? And to Maureen of all people.

Back in the room, I gathered my belongings and placed them where they could be easily packed, then went to the hotel to call A.P. I dreaded talking with her. I knew I had failed her miserably.

She picked up the telephone immediately. "Lacey, dear. How are you? The Homeland

Security agents told me about your experience. I will never forgive myself for sending you on that trip. You could have been killed." A.P. tended to talk fast without taking a breath.

"A.P." I interrupted. "I'm fine. I'm so sorry that I didn't protect AnnaLise and Hadley. They were dear people and I'm the reason they are dead."

"Now you stop that, Lacey. It is not your fault. According to all I've heard about Hadley's family, it would have happened whether in Ireland or here in the U.S."

"He really loved her A.P. They were happy together."

"Thanks for that, Lacey." I think she was crying. "Lacey, Homeland Security has made arrangements to fly them back on the same plane as you and Stella. I will see you at the airport."

I didn't realize Stella and I were on the same plane as the bodies, but when I checked the airline tickets McKinnon gave me after breakfast, I saw we were, indeed, routed through Atlanta, then back to St. Louis. Home, I'll be glad to get home.

Logan was waiting for me in the lobby. "I'm glad I caught you. Will you have lunch with me?"

"I don't think so." I tried to move around him.

He blocked my way. "Please. Lacey, by waiting for Kohane to show last night, we may have saved many lives. I'm sorry you were frightened. The pen had the information that was stolen, but Kohane and the others have the ability to strike the U.S. or Britain at any time. O'Shea and Irene are spilling their guts. We can put Kohane away for a long time.

"Please have lunch with me. No business allowed, just pleasure."

"I need to pick up a few things in Killarney. I was planning to go there for lunch."

"Are you still angry at me?"

"I'm still thinking about it."

We were silent as we drove into Killarney. He drove directly to a pub on one of the side streets. It was bright and homey, but crowded. We ordered sandwiches and coffee at the counter and found a table near a window.

"You don't follow the local custom of Guinness with lunch?" I asked.

"Drinking doesn't go with the job." His answer was short as he pulled out a chair for me. "Please don't be angry."

"I know you were doing your job. I'm still shaken up and disappointed that you let that happen to me."

"We needed to catch Kohane. If I thought you were in danger of losing your life, I would have rescued you in a minute. We have image-detecting equipment. I knew where you were every minute. I even saw you break up that chair to use as a weapon. I admire your resourcefulness."

"If you knew I had a weapon, why did you let me hit you with it?"

"I thought you could hear us arresting Bouchard and O'Shea. That is skinny guy's name, by the way. I was so anxious to get to you; I wasn't thinking that you would hit whoever came through the door.

"If it had been Kohane coming in the door, he

would have killed you. You know that don't you?"

"I knew they would kill me eventually. I didn't think they would kill me until they found the microchip. I figured I'd rather be killed fighting than just facing the gun, when they decided it was my time to go."

"I promised you not to talk business and here we are rehashing last night. Truce?"

"Truce."

"So when does your flight leave Shannon?"

"Around seven. Stella and I are flying to Atlanta with the bodies. I'm meeting AnnaLise's niece, A.P. there. She is also my agent. We have about two hours in Atlanta, then we catch a flight to St. Louis, then home. And you, when do you get back to the US?"

"I'll be here a few more days, winding up the case."

Logan was pleasant company, telling about his travels but I felt the weight of Maureen's ring in my pocket. Should I tell Logan about it? Would he feel he had to report to the local Guarda?

"Is something bothering you, Lacey?"

"No, I'm fine, still trying to wrap my head around what has happened."

"I know you are a writer, Lacey. I'll be looking for your books when I get back to the states."

I blushed. "My books will seem tame to you after your adventures on the job."

He smiled. "Sometimes tame is good. Tell me about your family.""Are you certain you want to get me started? I can talk about my children and grandchildren endlessly, but you know all about me.

You did a background check on me when you thought I was terrorist."

"I did. It was necessary. Everyone on the tour received the same scrutiny. You came up clean and your family also. I know they are solid citizens with jobs and responsibilities."

"I am blessed. My children and grandchildren are the absolute best. We have become even closer since my husband died. Tell me about your family?"

"The job doesn't allow much family time. My wife left me a long time ago and I do not have children."

"I'm sorry." My words just sort of hung there. What can you say to a man whose whole life is his job?

"There is a luggage store around here somewhere. Let's walk. What else do you need?"

"Suitcases for Stella and me. I want to buy more Tootsie Rolls, but nothing else today."

"Would you look at that?" He was gazing into the window of a toy store at a large green stuffed leprechaun. "My godchild would love that. He's three."

I laughed. He ducked into the store. I bought Tootsie Rolls and he bought the stuffed leprechaun.

"Tell, me Mr. G Man. How are you going to get that through customs?"

"I will carry it through and to heck what anyone thinks." We laughed and entered the luggage store.

"Just a couple of small bags with rollers. We don't have much left to take home."

"I'm sorry, Lacey." He wasn't laughing now.

Chapter 18

The bus was pulling in when Logan and I arrived back at Muckross Park Hotel. The sight of Rory helping Maureen off the bus hit me in the gut. I had her ring and I had to get it back to her without her knowledge. I didn't have a clue how to do that.

Logan leaned on the top of the car after unloading the suitcases. "I am glad to know you, Lacey. Here is my card. My personal phone number is on the back. Call me sometime."

"Thanks Logan. It was an experience I do not want to repeat. But maybe I'll call someday for pleasure, not for business." My smile was a little misty. It is hard to leave friends.

"You didn't give him your phone number," Stella said, as we walked away toward our room.

"He knows my phone number. In fact, he knows more about you and me than our children do." She looked at me in surprise.

"Background checks are very accurate."

"A background check, ummm! That makes me a little uncomfortable."

"Oh, relax, I doubt if he knows about the boy you kissed at the Senior Prom. But he certainly knows where you live and with whom you hang out. Did you have a nice lunch?" I asked Stella.

"Actually, Rory and I bought a sandwich and ate in the park." Did you eat?"

"Logan took me into Killarney and we had lunch and bought the suitcases. I bought you a Navy blue and the brown is mine. So will you be returning to Ireland or will Rory be visiting the states?"

"We'll see. I do have the voucher to return. Maybe you and I could return together. Of course, you may not want to come if Logan isn't here," she teased.

We walked off toward our room, trundling the suitcases behind us. "So you have forgiven Logan for last night."

"Yes, he was just doing his job. He really is a very caring man in a very demanding job.

"I've got a problem, Stella."

"You usually have a problem. Out with it."

By this time, we were safely in our room.

After locking the door, I took the ring out of my pocket.

"Is that what I think it is?" Stella was quick on the uptake. "I know you didn't steal it so where did you get it?"

I told her the whole story. "I don't have a clue how to return it to Maureen without her suspecting that I stole it. Better me than Rose, I guess. I don't think the poor old thing knew what she was doing."

Stella began to pack her suitcase. "Get your things together; we have to have the suitcases out in half-an-hour."

It didn't take long to throw the few items we had purchased into the suitcase. Then it struck me. "Oh darn, those goons destroyed the galleys and they were nearly finished."

"I'm sure A.P. can get you another copy."

"Sure but I'll have to do the corrections again. Did Logan tell you the pen had the microchip that all the fuss was about? Imagine that thing stuck in my purse while I carried it all over Ireland." I suddenly looked at Stella.

"Hey, that gives me an idea."

"You've got that look in your eye. Most of your ideas get you in trouble. What are you planning?"

"I'm not sure yet, but I'll make it happen."

We looked around the room for anything we left, then gathered up purses, carry bags and suitcases and left the Muckross Park Hotel.

We took a last look around. It was a beautiful place with much to offer. I was sorry to leave so soon but it had bad memories. I knew I couldn't return soon and enjoy it.

Rory was busy loading the suitcases into the belly of the bus as tour members gathered. I deposited my suitcase within Rory's reach and fingered the ring in my pocket. This was going to take some slight of hand. I prayed I could pull it off.

I crowded up behind Maureen as she made sure

she was first in line to board, bound for the front seat, no doubt. Stella shot me a puzzled look. I shrugged. Rory came around to hand us into the bus. As Maureen raised her foot for the first step, I threw the ring on the ground under her.

"Maureen, you dropped something." I stepped back and bent over as the ring rolled under the bus step. "There, see under the step."

Maureen stepped out of the bus and looked under the step. "My ring! It's my ring. How in the world did it get there?" She looked at me suspiciously.

"It must have been stuck in your clothing, maybe your jacket pocket."

"But I looked everywhere for it."

"Well, things like that happen sometimes. I'm glad you found it." I turned around to see Curtis collapse into a nearby chair. Stella ran to him.

He held up a hand. "I'm fine. No problem. Too much excitement. Thank you Stella." I knew he was talking to me.

Maureen slipped the ring on her finger. "Oh, I'm so glad to have my ring back. I thought it was gone forever. It was so sweet of Vernon to buy it for me and I thought someone stole it. What a coincidence to find it under the bus. Isn't it Vernon? What if we had boarded the bus without seeing it?" She was babbling.

"See Jo. My ring, it was stuck in my jacket, I guess and slipped out." She raised her hand to show everyone her ring. "I'm so glad I found it before I left Ireland."

Everyone crowded around to admire the ring,

including Rose. I breathed a sigh of relief. Like Curtis, I'd had enough excitement on this trip.

Epilogue

The plane trip to the US was an anticlimax to all that had happened in Ireland. We landed to sunny skies, but with heavy hearts as we met A.P. in Atlanta.

Stella and I stood respectively by A.P. as Hadley and AnnaLise were expertly handed into matching white hearses We bid farewell to an old couple who only expected a little love late in life.

A.P. turned to me, "Thanks again, Lacey. I'm more sorry than you know to have put you in harm's way. My mother and I are very grateful for your care and understanding."

"You didn't put me in harm's way, A.P. The danger was out there and I happened to be in the way. Another time and everything would have gone smoothly. Uh, one thing, A.P. the thugs who searched our room, destroyed the galleys. I'll need you to send them to me again."

"Oh, yes, that reminds me. I figured as much and brought a copy with me. It will give you something to do on the way home. I'll expect them back to me by the weekend."

About the Author

Pat lives and writes in the beautiful Missouri Ozarks. Her publication credits include Bible studies, articles, and short stories. She is a genealogist and has traced her family back to Germany and England. She photographs every old building and mill she sees and the family is sure the only pictures she takes while traveling are cemeteries. She loves to travel and often writes about her travels. Those settings and experiences usually end up in her stories.

Made in the USA
Charleston, SC
19 February 2015